目次 Contents

LISTENING TEST

Track-26

In the Listening test, you will be asked to demonstrate how well you understand spoken English. The entire Listening test will last approximately 45 minutes. There are four parts, and directions are given for each part. You must mark your answers on the separate answer sheet. Do not write your answers in your test book.

PART 1

Directions: For each question in this part, you will hear four statements about a picture in your test book. When you hear the statements, you must select the one statement that best describes what you see in the picture. Then find the number of the question on your answer sheet and mark your answer. The statements will not be printed in your test book and will be spoken only one time.

Statement (B), "They're shaking hands on the deal," is the best description of the picture, so you should select answer (B) and mark it on your answer sheet.

1.

2.

3.

GO ON TO THE NEXT PAGE →

4.

5.

6.

PART 2

Track-27

Directions: You will hear a question or statement and three responses spoken in English. They will not be printed in your test book and will be spoken only one time. Select the best response to the question or statement and mark the letter (A), (B), or (C) on your answer sheet.

7. Mark your answer on your answer sheet.
8. Mark your answer on your answer sheet.
9. Mark your answer on your answer sheet.
10. Mark your answer on your answer sheet.
11. Mark your answer on your answer sheet.
12. Mark your answer on your answer sheet.
13. Mark your answer on your answer sheet.
14. Mark your answer on your answer sheet.
15. Mark your answer on your answer sheet.
16. Mark your answer on your answer sheet.
17. Mark your answer on your answer sheet.
18. Mark your answer on your answer sheet.
19. Mark your answer on your answer sheet.
20. Mark your answer on your answer sheet.
21. Mark your answer on your answer sheet.
22. Mark your answer on your answer sheet.
23. Mark your answer on your answer sheet.
24. Mark your answer on your answer sheet.
25. Mark your answer on your answer sheet.
26. Mark your answer on your answer sheet.
27. Mark your answer on your answer sheet.
28. Mark your answer on your answer sheet.
29. Mark your answer on your answer sheet.
30. Mark your answer on your answer sheet.
31. Mark your answer on your answer sheet.

GO ON TO THE NEXT PAGE

PART 3

Directions: You will hear some conversations between two or more people. You will be asked to answer three questions about what the speakers say in each conversation. Select the best response to each question and mark the letter (A), (B), (C), or (D) on your answer sheet. The conversations will not be printed in your test book and will be spoken only one time.

32. Where does this conversation most likely take place?
    (A) In a record store
    (B) In a clothing store
    (C) In a convenience store
    (D) In a dry cleaner's

33. What is the problem?
    (A) The pink shirt is too big for the man.
    (B) The man wants to return the record.
    (C) The beverages all sold out.
    (D) The man can't find his shirt.

34. What does the woman suggest the man do?
    (A) Go to another store
    (B) Buy the shirt of medium size
    (C) Call the customer service
    (D) Choose a different color

35. What does the woman want to do?
    (A) Apply for membership of the gym
    (B) Work out in the gym
    (C) Ask the man out
    (D) Drive a car

36. Who is most likely the man?
    (A) A security guard
    (B) A trainer
    (C) A member of the gym
    (D) An employee of the gym

37. What does the man give the woman?
    (A) A new membership card
    (B) An identity card
    (C) A pass to use for today only
    (D) His phone number

6

38. What is true about the Runner A–5 Model?
(A) It is the latest model.
(B) The woman wants to buy it.
(C) The company has stopped producing it.
(D) The man can't find its manual.

39. What does the woman request?
(A) A catalog
(B) A link
(C) A new model
(D) An address

40. What will the woman most likely do next?
(A) Go to the store with her friend
(B) Select a new GPS model
(C) Check out her bank account
(D) Tell the man her e-mail address

41. What is the conversation mainly about?
(A) How to play baseball
(B) A baseball tournament
(C) Taiwan's baseball teams
(D) The speakers' favorite sports

42. Why does the man say, "No doubt about it"?
(A) He thinks the game must be great.
(B) He believes Japan is more likely to win.
(C) He is certain about the game time.
(D) He strongly disagrees with the women.

43. What does the man suggest?
(A) Buying tickets to tomorrow's game
(B) Talking about basketball
(C) Watching a game together
(D) Playing baseball this afternoon

44. What kind of service is provided by the man's company?
(A) Travel arrangements
(B) Web design
(C) Restaurant decoration
(D) Financial investment

45. When is the woman's appointment?
(A) Tomorrow
(B) This Friday
(C) This weekend
(D) Next week

46. What information is the woman asked to provide?
(A) When she is available
(B) Who recommended the services
(C) How much her budget is
(D) What she plans to do

47. What city are the speakers in now?
(A) San Francisco
(B) Boston
(C) Houston
(D) San Diego

48. Why is the restaurant busy now?
(A) It just moved to the downtown area.
(B) It has become very famous.
(C) The baseball season has begun.
(D) Many tourists have their holidays there.

49. Who will the man probably speak with next?
(A) The head chef
(B) A customer in the restaurant
(C) The hiring manager
(D) The owner of the restaurant

GO ON TO THE NEXT PAGE ➡

50. What do the speakers most likely work for?
    (A) A plant
    (B) The government
    (C) The Nelson Company
    (D) A construction company

51. Why has the construction work not begun?
    (A) The site is not safe.
    (B) The residents are delaying it.
    (C) The Nelson Company is short of funds.
    (D) The Nelson Company has changed their plan.

52. When will the meeting take place?
    (A) At 7:30 a.m. this Tuesday
    (B) At 7:30 this evening
    (C) At 7:30 p.m. next Tuesday
    (D) At 7:30 a.m. next Thursday

53. What is the conversation mainly about?
    (A) A vacation in Dubai
    (B) A trip to London
    (C) A convention in Sydney
    (D) A car rental company

54. What is the problem that the speakers find?
    (A) They can't afford the rent.
    (B) No one has arranged ground transportation yet.
    (C) There is no shuttle bus service from the airport to their hotel.
    (D) They forgot to reserve plane tickets.

55. What will the man most likely do next?
    (A) Cancel the trip
    (B) Book air tickets
    (C) Talk to some famous people
    (D) Call the car rental company

56. What is the woman's problem?
    (A) She needs a new digital camera.
    (B) She can't find the battery she needs.
    (C) The battery she needs is too expensive.
    (D) Her camera needs to be fixed.

57. What does the man say about the woman's digital camera?
    (A) It is an older model.
    (B) It is out of stock.
    (C) It is beyond repair.
    (D) It is a valuable antique.

58. What will the woman most likely do next?
    (A) Go to another store to look for the battery she needs
    (B) Get into an argument with the man
    (C) Purchase a battery online
    (D) Give the man her phone number

59. Who are most likely the speakers?
    (A) Cleaners
    (B) Office workers
    (C) Sales clerks
    (D) Drivers

60. When will the cleaning most likely take place?
    (A) Monday or Tuesday
    (B) Tuesday or Wednesday
    (C) Thursday or Friday
    (D) Saturday or Sunday

61. What is the woman probably going to do next?
    (A) Clean the office
    (B) Talk to her boss
    (C) Call the cleaning company
    (D) Get back to work

62. What is the problem?

(A) Customers are complaining about the milk.

(B) The man is taking too many phone calls.

(C) The woman is not satisfied with the milk.

(D) The store is going to close down.

63. What do the speakers think the cause of the problem may be?

(A) The supplier sends them products of poor quality.

(B) The business is getting worse.

(C) There might be something wrong with the freezer.

(D) Too many colleagues are off today.

64. How will the man solve the problem?

(A) He will use a new way to promote the milk.

(B) He will contact a technician.

(C) He will apologize to the customers.

(D) He will call the HR manager.

Extra Charges
■ Meal: $15
■ Stroller (checked): $10
■ Seat selection: $30
■ Small pets (in cage): $25
■ Change booking: $50

65. Where does the woman most likely work?

(A) At a train station

(B) At a pet store

(C) At a travel agency

(D) At a department store

66. Why is the man calling?

(A) To cancel his railway reservation

(B) To book a plane ticket

(C) To buy a small pet dog

(D) To inquire about the anniversary sale

67. Look at the graphic. How much should the man pay additionally?

(A) $25

(B) $50

(C) $15

(D) $30

Time	Activities
7:30—8:00——Breakfast	
8:10——Go to the city of Ace	
9:10—10:00——**312 Museum**	
10:10—11:00——**Peace Cathedral**	
11:10—12:00——**Monument Park**	
12:00—13:30——Lunch	
13:30—14:20——**Happy Opera House**	
14:30—15:30——**Bond Street** (shopping)	
15:30——Go back to the hotel	

68. Where does the woman want to stay longer?

(A) 312 Museum

(B) Monument Park

(C) Happy Opera House

(D) Bond Street

69. Look at the graphic. When will the speakers go back to the hotel?

(A) 3:30 p.m.

(B) 4:30 p.m.

(C) 5:30 p.m.

(D) 6:30 p.m.

70. What does the man prefer to buy?

(A) Clothes

(B) Computers

(C) Windows

(D) Nothing

GO ON TO THE NEXT PAGE

PART 4

Directions: You will hear some talks given by a single speaker. You will be asked to answer three questions about what the speaker says in each talk. Select the best response to each question and mark the letter (A), (B), (C), or (D) on your answer sheet. The talks will not be printed in your test book and will be spoken only one time.

71. Where does the speaker most likely work?
    (A) A hotel
    (B) A travel agency
    (C) An airline
    (D) A youth hostel

72. Where will the customer travel to?
    (A) Paris
    (B) Taipei
    (C) Bangkok
    (D) Tokyo

73. What does the speaker suggest the listener do?
    (A) Contact the office
    (B) Cancel the booking
    (C) Give 44 names
    (D) Change the itinerary

74. When is the announcement being made?
    (A) In the early morning
    (B) At lunchtime
    (C) In the afternoon
    (D) In the evening

75. How long did preparing for the exhibition take?
    (A) One semester
    (B) Three months
    (C) One year
    (D) Three weeks

76. What does the speaker say about the artists?
    (A) They are French.
    (B) Their works are original.
    (C) Their works express their thoughts.
    (D) People can learn about their culture through the photos.

10

77. What is the speaker concerned about?

(A) Water pollution

(B) Global warming

(C) An energy crisis

(D) An economic issue

78. What does the speaker advise listeners to do?

(A) Drive an electric car to work

(B) Pay attention to the current economic climate

(C) Use energy-efficient light bulbs

(D) Reduce the use of detergent

79. What does the speaker mean when saying "if we all pitch in"?

(A) Everyone should do something for the earth.

(B) The government should adopt the right policy.

(C) Listeners should join the protest march.

(D) People should try to pitch the stone into the space.

80. What is the message about?

(A) A long vacation

(B) A business trip

(C) An annual company trip

(D) A summer camp

81. Which of the following countries will Alan NOT go to?

(A) Thailand

(B) Hong Kong

(C) India

(D) Indonesia

82. What does the speaker ask for?

(A) Ground transportation information

(B) Passport number and the name on the passport

(C) The names of the clients

(D) The phone number of the travel agent

83. What is the speaker's job?

(A) A television reporter

(B) A video game salesperson

(C) A game reviewer

(D) A store manager

84. Which of the following is NOT true?

(A) The new game has been reviewed favorably.

(B) The graphics of the new game are better than its old version's.

(C) There are a lot of people waiting in line to buy the game.

(D) The new game is given away today.

85. What does the speaker say many parents may have difficulty doing?

(A) Putting their children to bed

(B) Entertaining their children

(C) Stopping their children from using their cell phones

(D) Asking their children to do their homework

86. Which country seems to have no room for increasing sales?

(A) South Africa   (B) Nigeria

(C) The USA   (D) Morocco

87. What is the problem with the Chinese market?

(A) There are no branch offices in China.

(B) Sales in China have been stagnant for several years.

(C) People there are not interested in luxury goods.

(D) Its government makes it hard to promote the products there.

88. In which area is the company going to open new branch offices this year?

(A) India   (B) America

(C) Europe   (D) Africa

GO ON TO THE NEXT PAGE

89. What is the purpose of the message?

(A) To make a request

(B) To express gratitude

(C) To offer congratulations

(D) To give some advice

90. What did Takashi help prepare at the party?

(A) The music

(B) The invitations

(C) The dishes

(D) The decorations

91. What does the speaker hope that Takashi will do on Monday?

(A) Prepare for another party

(B) Have dinner with her

(C) Start to teach her Japanese

(D) Bring some sushi rolls

92. Who is the announcement for?

(A) Park rangers

(B) Tourists

(C) Bus drivers

(D) Security guards

93. Why are two of the trails marked "off limits"?

(A) There are dangerous snakes there.

(B) The trails are too difficult for novice hikers.

(C) Landslides happened there recently.

(D) There are infected mosquitoes there.

94. What does the speaker give to the listeners?

(A) Bug repellent

(B) Maps

(C) Pesticide

(D) Bottled water

Be Super Productive at Work
10:00–10:30 Welcome and Introduction
10:30–12:00 **Essential Time Management Skills**
12:00–13:00 Lunch
13:00–14:30 **Be Focused**
14:30–15:30 Breakout Session
15:30–17:00 **Be Happy as You Can Be**

95. What does the speaker say about the workshop?

(A) It offers refreshments during the breakout session.

(B) People should sign up as soon as possible.

(C) The speakers will give useful advice.

(D) Attendees need to fill out a comment card online.

96. Look at the graphic. When are the consultant meetings offered?

(A) 10:30–12:00

(B) 12:00–13:00

(C) 13:00–14:30

(D) 14:30–15:30

97. Where can listeners find the agenda?

(A) A brochure

(B) A poster

(C) A website

(D) A bulletin board

New Office Equipment Inventory
■ Desks: 8
■ Chairs: 12
■ Telephones: 2
■ Fax machines: 1
■ Computers: 8
■ Printers: 2

98. Who is most likely the speaker?

(A) Product manager

(B) Accounting manager

(C) Warehouse manager

(D) General affairs manager

99. How many workers are expected to use the new office?

(A) 5

(B) 6

(C) 10

(D) 11

100. Look at the graphic. What will Alison have to order for the new office?

(A) One chair

(B) One fax machine

(C) Two desks

(D) Two printers

This is the end of the Listening test. Turn to Part 5 in your test book.

READING TEST

In the Reading test, you will read a variety of texts and answer several different types of reading comprehension questions. The entire Reading test will last 75 minutes. There are three parts, and directions are given for each part. You are encouraged to answer as many questions as possible within the time allowed.

You must mark your answers on the separate answer sheet. Do not write your answers in your test book.

PART 5

Directions: A word or phrase is missing in each of the sentences below. Four answer choices are given below each sentence. Select the best answer to complete the sentence. Then mark the letter (A), (B), (C), or (D) on your answer sheet.

101. Sally should arrive ten minutes before ------- supervisor arrives.
(A) herself
(B) she
(C) her
(D) hers

102. The ------- delights of France are very well-known in the world.
(A) culinary
(B) beneficial
(C) lingering
(D) bizarre

103. Mr. Anderson's company sells ------- low-priced goods and luxury goods.
(A) every
(B) both
(C) either
(D) not only

104. Neil Adams ------- by the chairman as chief executive officer.
(A) nominated
(B) to nominate
(C) was nominating
(D) was nominated

105. A live coverage of the NBA Finals will ------- begin.
(A) ever
(B) soon
(C) yet
(D) since

106. The tour guide advised that the tourists not ------- out alone in this area at night.
(A) went
(B) to go
(C) go
(D) going

107. The rainstorm came ------- than expected, and we got drenched.
(A) earlier
(B) early
(C) earliness
(D) earliest

108. Because of the sudden snowstorm, the store opened at 11:30 a.m. ------- 10:00 a.m. today.
(A) in spite of
(B) instead of
(C) regardless of
(D) because of

14

109. The ------- of the plane was delayed due to the strong wind at the airport.
(A) depart
(B) departed
(C) departing
(D) departure

110. Josh would rather do the task on his own than ------- with his colleagues.
(A) cooperate
(B) cooperated
(C) cooperation
(D) cooperative

111. We are confident that our team has a ------- good chance of winning the contract.
(A) rarely
(B) none
(C) very
(D) far

112. If you have already paid the entry fee, ------- no other payment is required.
(A) though
(B) then
(C) even
(D) but

113. Are you sure that the small church hall can ------- two hundred guests?
(A) adhere
(B) accommodate
(C) accelerate
(D) acquaint

114. Nowadays, people can't live without ------- lights in their daily lives.
(A) electronic
(B) electricity
(C) electric
(D) electronics

115. We need to modify the plan because our clients won't arrive ------- tomorrow.
(A) despite
(B) unless
(C) upon
(D) until

116. Joshua Roberts is the ------- to Bella Watson as president of the company.
(A) authority
(B) successor
(C) ancestor
(D) descendant

117. The company is trying to expand its business ------- Southeast Asia.
(A) along
(B) between
(C) into
(D) with

118. The researchers in the laboratory have developed a ------- for detecting the defective genes in the human body.
(A) method
(B) symptom
(C) therapy
(D) distribution

119. As a successful actor -------, Justin Reeves understands how hard it is to act well.
(A) he
(B) himself
(C) him
(D) his

120. The manager appreciates the ------- we made to developing this new product.
(A) contributors
(B) contributory
(C) contributes
(D) contributions

GO ON TO THE NEXT PAGE

121. Management encouraged the sales department to ------- the sales performance of last year.
(A) bargain
(B) minimize
(C) notify
(D) surpass

122. The citizens of the city are looking forward to the ------- of the new metro line.
(A) complete
(B) completion
(C) completely
(D) completed

123. The fans were very excited ------- they waited for their turn to get their idol's autograph.
(A) as
(B) or
(C) except
(D) whereas

124. Those who want to know the details about the project can ask Sarah Smith in the meeting or send ------- an e-mail any time this week.
(A) she
(B) their
(C) her
(D) they

125. Even though most people thought Mr. Rivera was too ------- for the job, it turned out that he was a very good choice.
(A) additional
(B) probable
(C) inexperienced
(D) believable

126. We will need to review all of your email ------- with the clients to make sure you are competent at communicating.
(A) correspond
(B) correspondent
(C) corresponding
(D) correspondence

127. Microwave ovens and refrigerators are very common household ------- in a modern kitchen.
(A) conditions
(B) appliances
(C) terminals
(D) remains

128. ------- you have signed up for the course, it is impossible to cancel your registration.
(A) Once
(B) Always
(C) Regarding
(D) Whether

129. The snow ------- on the roads has caused many problems for the drivers and pedestrians.
(A) sanction
(B) duration
(C) accumulation
(D) procedure

130. ------- you are unable to arrive on time, please call us in advance.
(A) After
(B) If
(C) Besides
(D) Meanwhile

PART 6

Directions: Read the texts that follow. A word, phrase, or sentence is missing in parts of each text. Four answer choices for each question are given below the text. Select the best answer to complete the text. Then mark the letter (A), (B), (C), or (D) on your answer sheet.

Questions 131–134 refer to the following letter.

Dear Mr. Jones,

I would like to thank you for your order of our air quality monitor. Nowadays, more and more people are concerned ------- the quality of the air they breathe and want to take control of this. Unfortunately,
131.
although the model of the monitor you ordered is in stock, the gray ones you requested are out of stock at the moment. -------. If you would like, you can choose a ------- color for immediate delivery.
132. **133.**
The other options are black, white, blue and red. Or you can wait for one more month. Please -------
134.
to this letter at your earliest convenience with your decision.

Sincerely,

Jessica Flint
CGI Technologies Customer Service

131. (A) of
 (B) about
 (C) on
 (D) with

132. (A) We won't have any more gray models in the future.
 (B) We don't plan to sell them again in the future.
 (C) It will probably be about one month before we receive another shipment.
 (D) You can choose any model you like from our catalog.

133. (A) suitable
 (B) brilliant
 (C) vivid
 (D) different

134. (A) reply
 (B) demand
 (C) wait
 (D) delete

GO ON TO THE NEXT PAGE

Questions 135–138 refer to the following notice.

The work at two of the stations on the Green Line ------- disruptions to rail services for the next two
135.
weeks. South Street and Smith Street stations will be closed for the two weeks. ------- the trains will
136.
continue to operate, they may be delayed at times due to the work. If it is possible for you to take

another line to your -------, it is highly recommended that you consider alternative routes. -------. We
137.   138.
hope the enhanced services that result from the work will compensate for this.

135. (A) caused
(B) causes
(C) will cause
(D) was causing

136. (A) While
(B) Except
(C) Whenever
(D) Despite

137. (A) goal
(B) destination
(C) purpose
(D) achievement

138. (A) They will work hard to get a bonus.
(B) The work will be finished earlier than scheduled.
(C) We apologize for the inconvenience.
(D) It will happen during the next two weeks.

18

Questions 139–142 refer to the following article.

Welcome to the city, all the runners. As the mayor, it is a pleasure and an honor for me to see you run in our marathon. -------. All of the members of our community wish you the best as you make your

139.

42.2-kilometer run through the city.

While you are staying here, you can also take the ------- to visit the attractions of the city. We have a

140.

world-famous zoo and a beautiful waterfront with a shopping arcade and many restaurants -------

141.

various local specialties. -------, our art gallery is also worth a visit. It has a huge collection of modern

142.

art.

Thank you so much for coming. I wish your stay a pleasant one and your marathon a success.

139. (A) You need to pay the registration fee.
(B) I encourage you to stay longer in our city.
(C) This is an event that we take pride in.
(D) Let me explain why we hold the race.

140. (A) perspective
(B) opportunity
(C) qualification
(D) responsibility

141. (A) serving
(B) served
(C) serve
(D) server

142. (A) Specifically
(B) Additionally
(C) Even so
(D) Until then

GO ON TO THE NEXT PAGE

Roger Foster
Robinson Engineering Corp.
21 Ford Avenue
Montreal, Quebec

Dear Mr. Foster,

On behalf of everyone on the competition committee, I would like ------- you on qualifying for Canada
143.
Industrial Design Competition. Only the best designers from all over Canada are able to qualify for

the competition. Your ------- is a great honor to both you and your company.
144.

It is highly challenging to beat out the other best industrial designers. -------. On November 22, you
145.
will have to give a presentation in Edmonton to show the model of your design. Enclosed with this

letter is the information that you will need to reserve plane tickets ------- accommodations in
146.
Edmonton. If you need any assistance, please do not hesitate to send me an e-mail.

Best regards,

Joseph Basil
Competition Committee Member
Canada Industrial Design Competition

143. (A) congratulate
(B) congratulates
(C) to congratulate
(D) congratulations

144. (A) priority
(B) motion
(C) representative
(D) accomplishment

145. (A) We wish you the best of luck.
(B) I have expended so much effort.
(C) They have to face the challenge.
(D) Please arrange the ground transportation.

146. (A) in spite of
(B) as well as
(C) because of
(D) compared to

PART 7

Directions: In this part you will read a selection of texts, such as magazine and newspaper articles, e-mails, and instant messages. Each text or set of texts is followed by several questions. Select the best answer for each question and mark the letter (A), (B), (C), or (D) on your answer sheet.

Questions 147–148 refer to the following advertisement.

Part-time Cook Wanted

Darren's Steakhouse is looking for a part-time cook. No experience is needed. All we are looking for is someone who has a work ethic, is willing to learn and has a lot of energy to devote in a very busy kitchen. Must be available two or three evenings each week plus weekends. It is a perfect job for a student. We have flexible schedules. Above all, we offer high pay and a big bonus for our employees. For those interested, please apply in person to our kitchen manager at our Main Street location.

147. How much work experience is needed to apply for the job?
(A) None
(B) Six months
(C) One year
(D) Two years

148. Which of the following is NOT true about the job?
(A) The cook may need to work on weekends.
(B) The working environment is busy.
(C) The pay is good.
(D) The schedule is fixed.

GO ON TO THE NEXT PAGE

Questions 149–150 refer to the following text message chain.

Sally Moore   15:22

Are you going to the international conference this Saturday?

- -

Andrew Martin   15:22

Yes.

- -

Sally Moore   15:23

Are you available after the conference? I'd like to talk about the new project.

- -

Andrew Martin   15:24

Sure. The conference ends at noon, and my flight leaves at 3:30 p.m. We may go to lunch together and discuss.

- -

Sally Moore   15:25

Good idea. I can make lunch reservations at a restaurant there.

- -

Andrew Martin   15:25

Thanks!

- -

Sally Moore   15:26

See you on Saturday.

| send |

149. What is suggested about Mr. Martin?

(A) He will not attend the conference.

(B) His flight leaves in the evening.

(C) He will discuss a project with Ms. Moore.

(D) He is going to make lunch reservations.

150. When is the conference?

(A) This Saturday afternoon

(B) This Saturday morning

(C) This Saturday evening

(D) This Saturday night

Questions 151–152 refer to the following order form.

Barbara's Clothing Alteration Shop

Order Number: BE–354

Drop-off date: July 9

Customer: Albert Davis

Contact number: 0911123456

Item: A yellow jersey

Alteration: Embroider the words "Albert Davis" and "100th Marathon" on the jersey

Color of words: Blue

Pick-up date: July 25

Alteration assigned to: Susan Swade

---

151. What does Albert Davis want to alter?

(A) A suit he wears when diving

(B) A jacket he wears when skiing

(C) A shirt he wears when running

(D) A sweater he wears when hiking

152. Who most likely is Susan Swade?

(A) A runner

(B) A tailor

(C) A driver

(D) A painter

GO ON TO THE NEXT PAGE →

Questions 153–154 refer to the following e-mail.

✉	

From: Amanda Black <ablack@activeclothing.com>

To: Frank Sampson <fsampson@appleton.com>

Re: T-shirts

Date: September 17

Dear Mr. Sampson,

Thank you for your inquiry about purchasing T-shirts from our company. We guarantee the quality of our T-shirts as well as the graphic design you wish to be placed on your team's T-shirts. Please look at our price list below, and let me know what your team would like. Please be specific about the sleeve type, design, color and size that you require in your order.

Sleeve Type	Color
Long-sleeve T-shirts: $12 per unit	Red, yellow, blue, white, black, green
Short-sleeve T-shirts: $8 per unit	Others: _____
	Size
Design	XS: _____ units S: _____ units
In-house design: $70 per hour of work*	M: _____ units L: _____ units
On T-shirt: $2 per unit	XL: _____ units

*Not required. Customers can provide the design on their own.

Note: 1. Customers are allowed a 10% discount on orders over 50 units.

      2. There will be extra shipping charges.

      3. Local tax will be added if applicable.

If you have any questions, please feel free to ask.

Sincerely,

Amanda Black

Group Sales

Active Clothing, Inc.

153. Why does Ms. Black write this e-mail?

(A) To make a complaint about a product

(B) To send information to a potential buyer

(C) To place an order for a T-shirt

(D) To recruit a new employee

154. What is the customer allowed to provide?

(A) The shirts

(B) The equipment

(C) The discount

(D) The design

Questions 155–157 refer to the following article.

Los Angeles (July 15) — Cookie Fantastic is introducing a new flavor of cookies in the California market at the end of this month. Milk tea-flavored cream filling will feature in this new line of cookies.

The company president Adrian Meldane noted that there is a large Asian-American population in the state and that many of them like products with a milk tea flavor. He also noted the popularity of milk tea in the broader Los Angeles community as well as Asian communities. — [1] —. The popularity of milk tea flavored ice cream by another local company has also convinced the president of the possible success of the new product. The company has conducted taste tests over the past four months. — [2] —. The filling will be offered on a trial basis in California markets for two months. After those two months, future decisions about expanding the product will be made. — [3] —.

Meldane said, "We all know that the Angelino community is diverse and that Asian flavors are becoming increasingly popular in our community. — [4] —. We strongly believe that this flavor will similarly meet with success and will prove popular."

155. What is indicated about Cookie Fantastic?
(A) It is introducing a new line of cookies.
(B) It was founded by Adrian Meldane.
(C) It is the largest cookie company in Los Angeles.
(D) It specializes in Asian flavored products.

156. Which of the following was NOT noted by Adrian Meldane?
(A) There are many Asian Americans in California.
(B) Milk tea ice cream has already very popular.
(C) Milk tea flavored cookies are very popular in California.
(D) Milk tea is also popular outside the Asian-American community.

157. In which of the positions marked [1], [2], [3], and [4] does the following sentence best belong?

"These tests showed that people of all backgrounds liked milk tea-flavored cream filling."
(A) [1]
(B) [2]
(C) [3]
(D) [4]

GO ON TO THE NEXT PAGE

Questions 158–160 refer to the following memo.

To: All staff members
From: Human resources
Date: November 1

It has come to management's attention that too many employees are exceeding the limit of 30 minutes for their lunch break. Management would like to remind employees that when they take more time than scheduled for their lunch break, it would prevent their colleagues from taking their own break. It also reduces the efficiency with which we run the various departments throughout the supermarket.

Management is aware that outside the supermarket there are not many places to buy lunch. Thus, two measures are being taken to solve this problem. One of them is that a refrigerator and a microwave oven will be placed in the common room. All employees are welcome to use them. However, the employees' names must be clearly marked on all the food and drinks kept in the refrigerator. Besides, no food should be kept in the refrigerator overnight without the front end manager's permission.

The second measure is that food will be ordered from a local restaurant daily for any interested employees. The daily menu will be posted in the common room every morning. Employees merely need to write down the food they'd like to order and pay the front end manager for what they order prior to lunchtime.

And as always, any food items in our supermarket can be purchased with the usual 25% employee discount. We thank you for your cooperation and help in making our supermarket the best in the area.

Chloe Morgan

158. What is the problem mentioned in the memo?

(A) The employees can't get anything to eat at lunchtime.

(B) There aren't enough employees to carry out all the work.

(C) Many employees' lunch breaks are longer than scheduled.

(D) Some employees often forget to pay for their lunch.

159. According to the memo, what CAN'T the employees do without the front end manager's permission?

(A) Go outside the supermarket to buy lunch

(B) Order food from a restaurant nearby

(C) Use the microwave oven in the common room

(D) Leave their food in the refrigerator overnight

160. Who most likely is Chloe Morgan?

(A) A front end manager

(B) A human resources manager

(C) A purchasing manager

(D) A cafeteria manager

GO ON TO THE NEXT PAGE

Questions 161–164 refer to the following online discussion.

Ethan: [13:22] What is the status of the order from Mr. Lin?

Zoe: [13:26] Are you talking about the shipment of paint supplies to Taiwan?

Ethan: [13:28] Yes. The computer shows that it hasn't been sent out yet, though we received the order on the 12th.

Zoe: [13:32] The paints were prepared four days ago, on the 22nd. The order hasn't been sent out yet? Perhaps Lucas knows what the problem is.

Lucas: [13:37] I just identified the problem. Mr. Lin also wanted six kinds of art paper, but two of them were out of stock. However, we just received a large shipment from our supplier today. The workers at the docks are unloading it right now. According to the shipping label, what Mr. Lin needs should be in this shipment.

Ethan: [13:40] If they are in this shipment, when can we expect to send out the order? Mr. Lin wants to know the time.

Lucas: [13:45] Assuming everything else is set to go, it should be ready by 6 or 7 p.m.

Zoe: [13:49] The boxes are ready. We can ship them out immediately when the art paper arrives.

---

161. What kind of business are the three people probably working for?

(A) A shipping company

(B) An art supplies company

(C) A textile factory

(D) An art gallery

162. When was the order received?

(A) Two weeks ago

(B) Three weeks ago

(C) Four days ago

(D) Ten days ago

163. Why was the order delayed?

(A) The weather was bad.

(B) The order form was missing.

(C) Mr. Lin made some changes to his order.

(D) Two kinds of art paper were out of stock.

164. After the discussion, when is the order expected to be sent out?

(A) Right now

(B) This evening

(C) Tomorrow

(D) Next week

Questions 165–167 refer to the following notice.

Computer Lab Rules

1. Show your card to a librarian for the password.

2. Food and drinks are not allowed in the lab.

3. No one can use a computer for more than one hour.

4. Don't download any software or applications.

5. Take off your shoes before entering the lab.

6. Respect other users by using headphones and keeping the volume low.

165. Where most likely is the notice posted?

(A) At a train station

(B) At a bookstore

(C) At a public library

(D) At a shopping mall

166. Which of the following behaviors is acceptable in the computer lab?

(A) Drinking tea

(B) Downloading a game

(C) Watching a video with headphones

(D) Wearing one's shoes

167. What is the longest time one can use the computer for?

(A) 30 minutes

(B) 60 minutes

(C) Two hours

(D) Three hours

GO ON TO THE NEXT PAGE

Questions 168–171 refer to the following e-mail

From: Thomas Cooper <fitnesscourse@unbelievable.com>

To: Callie Scott <callie7931@pmail.com>

Subject: Congratulations

Date: June 30

Hello,

Unbelievable Fitness Center would like to congratulate you on finishing our fitness course this month! We believe that you have learned, grown, and become healthier and stronger. We are glad to witness your change. Please fill out a feedback form for us: http://unbelievable.fitnesscourse/feedback-form, so that we will know what you think about our course and our fitness center. You will get a free sports towel if you fill out the form before July 1.

To keep fit is never easy. We hope that the end of this course will not be the end of your training but another beginning. If you want to be a robust person, please keep following us. Our next fitness course will begin on July 8. Please register by July 5. We will again provide you with adequate exercise and careful instruction. And since you are already a member of our center, you are entitled to 15% off the next course!

If you have any questions about the new course, do not hesitate to contact us. It is always our desire to see all our members live a healthy and happy life. Please let us be your lifelong workout companion.

Sincerely,

Thomas Cooper
Unbelievable Fitness Center

168. What is the purpose of the e-mail?

(A) To advertise a job opportunity

(B) To promote a new fitness course

(C) To give advice on how to exercise

(D) To encourage those who want to lose weight

169. The word "robust" in paragraph 2, line 2, is closest in meaning to

(A) cheerful

(B) slender

(C) healthy

(D) promising

170. What is indicated about Callie Scott?

(A) She has filled out the feedback form.

(B) She has the membership of the fitness center.

(C) She is looking for an exercise partner.

(D) She has not taken any fitness course before.

171. When is the deadline for the registration?

(A) June 30

(B) July 1

(C) July 5

(D) July 8

GO ON TO THE NEXT PAGE

Greeneville Publisher
328 Maple Street, Springfield,
Massachusetts 01101
(820) 624–7800

Cameron Russell
302 Central Street
Manchester, New Hampshire 03103

Dear Mr. Russell,

We are pleased that you are considering placing your order with our company. — [1] —. Plenty of our language learning books have won various awards, and our series on learning French have earned the praise of many readers worldwide. All of the writers, illustrators, designers, and staff here take great pride in the work that we have done. — [2] —.

You will find that lots of our books have been updated in the past two years, ensuring that they contain the latest information and employ the latest language learning methods. In addition, most of the books include a variety of learning activities. — [3] —. There are also numerous supplemental resources that are available, including workbooks, DVDs, CD-ROM, and online tutorials.

Please look at the guide I have enclosed. — [4] —. I am sure it will help you as you choose which books to buy. I also encourage you to visit our website to see the demonstrations of the variety of audiovisual learning aids. If you have any further questions, please do not hesitate to call us or send us an e-mail.

Kind regards,

Harper Powell
Greeneville Publisher

172. What is the purpose of the letter?

(A) To invite a writer to write new books

(B) To provide information on books

(C) To advertise for new teachers

(D) To boast about the achievements of the publisher

173. What is enclosed with the letter?

(A) An employment contract

(B) An order form

(C) A sample of a book

(D) A guide to the books

174. The word "employ" in paragraph 2, line 2, is closest in meaning to

(A) use

(B) hire

(C) invent

(D) change

175. In which of the positions marked [1], [2], [3], and [4] does the following sentence best belong?

"They are all designed to stimulate learners of different levels to learn and think."

(A) [1]

(B) [2]

(C) [3]

(D) [4]

GO ON TO THE NEXT PAGE

CHIESA Supply

Client Name: James Thompson

Client Address: 794 Mains Road, Sunnybank Hills, Brisbane

Date: May 12

Item number	Description	Quantity	Unit Price (AUD)	Total (AUD)
RT 19855	Blue and white rug 195 cm × 250 cm	1,500	$100	$150,000
RT 19854	Queen sized bed 152 cm × 203 cm	20	$300	$6,000
RT 19853	Side table 55 cm × 55 cm × 45 cm	140	$120	$16,800
RT 19852	Assembled pier table 45 cm × 60 cm × 55 cm	130	$130	$16,900
Total				$189,700

✉

To:	thompson@sevenstarhotel.com
From:	gonzales@chiesasupply.com
Subject:	Apology for the problems with Mr. Thompson's order
Date:	May 15

Dear Mr. Thompson,

We have an apology to make to you. We learned that there are some problems with the items delivered to your hotel: the rugs are four less than you ordered, and the components of five of the assembled pier tables are damaged. We apologize for these problems.

We sent you the four rugs this morning. As for the components, we are sorry to tell you they are out of stock and that the pier tables have been discontinued. We will refund the full price of the five tables.

If you have any questions about your order, please do not hesitate to contact us.

Yours sincerely,

Andrea Gonzales
Sales Representative
07–1234–5678
CHIESA Supply

176. Why did Ms. Gonzales write to Mr. Thompson?

(A) To order some furniture

(B) To promote new products

(C) To make an apology

(D) To request information

177. When were the four rugs sent to Mr. Thompson's hotel?

(A) Yesterday

(B) This morning

(C) This afternoon

(D) Tonight

178. What is suggested about the pier tables?

(A) The components are not available.

(B) They were damaged by the driver.

(C) They are being manufactured.

(D) They were delivered to the wrong place.

179. How much will CHIESA Supply refund Mr. Thompson?

(A) $400

(B) $520

(C) $600

(D) $650

180. What is the size of the rug?

(A) 45 cm × 60 cm

(B) 55 cm × 55 cm

(C) 152 cm × 203 cm

(D) 195 cm × 250 cm

GO ON TO THE NEXT PAGE

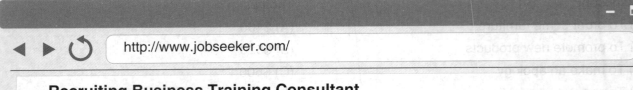

Recruiting Business Training Consultant

Name of company: Hiller Heiman

Position: A large scale international business is looking for an experienced businessman to take on the position of business trainer and consultant.

Requirements for applicants: Applicants need to be diligent workers and researchers, be dependable in their work ethics, and be good at handling interpersonal relationships with clients.

Job content: The job includes speaking at large training events and guiding and motivating entrepreneurs to successfully launch a company. The consultant will have to participate in internal training courses (i.e. on-the-job training) once a month and organize external training programs for businessmen.

Start date: Within one week

Dear Hiring Manager,

My name is Johnny McBeth. I am writing to apply for the position of Business Training Consultant that was advertised in the newspaper this month.

My experience in the relevant fields is as follows: I have 15 years of experience working in a trading business in Shanghai City. I was once a sales representative for Hong Kong Shanghai Trading Company Limited, which was a local Chinese enterprise that exported software to Hong Kong. After working there for three years, I was then promoted to manager. I had also worked as a part-time business consultant for ten years. I organized workshops and ran business training courses for local businesses.

I am confident that I can take on this position and ensure that your business training courses and workshops best profit your clients. If I am found suitable for this position, please contact me by next Thursday, April 12, at the latest. I will only be available for the interview by then.

Thank you very much.

Johnny McBeth

181. What is suggested about Hiller Heiman?

(A) It is based in Shanghai City.

(B) It offers business training programs.

(C) It is hiring a sales representative.

(D) Most of its clients are secretaries.

182. According to the web page, what is the successful applicant required to do?

(A) Help export software to Hong Kong

(B) Speak at large business expositions

(C) Participate in international conferences

(D) Give advice on how to start a business

183. What probably makes Mr. McBeth suitable for the position?

(A) He used to work as a researcher.

(B) He is an experienced construction worker.

(C) He has lots of experience in business consultation.

(D) He handled shipping in a trading company.

184. If Mr. McBeth is hired, when does he most likely start to work?

(A) In April

(B) In May

(C) In June

(D) In July

185. In the letter, the word "available" in paragraph 3, line 3, is closest in meaning to

(A) easy

(B) free

(C) handy

(D) accessible

GO ON TO THE NEXT PAGE

A Happy Rabbit and *The Lord of Donuts*   by Hazel Tryniski

◆ *A Happy Rabbit*: A rabbit decides to be a happy rabbit after seeing human beings' happiness and sorrows. In this story, all pets can talk, and they always make witty remarks.

◆*The Lord of Donuts*: Dominic is a baker. One day he meets a stranger who takes him to a mysterious kingdom, where he goes on an incredible magical journey.

PG2 Radio

Prime-Time Broadcast Schedule
Tuesday, March 27

18:00 – **Sports Tonight**: The most popular sports talk show in town. Join our host Ryan Jackson as he talks about sports with some outstanding athletes and other guests in the local sports field.

19:00 – **Author's Corner**: This evening's guest, Carson Tryniski, will tell us what he thinks about his mother's two novels. He will also talk about the compilation and publication of his mother's background notes about the fictional setting of the novels.

20:00 – **Let's Talk About Politics**: Sean Watson will talk about local politics. Listen and call in. Let our city hear your voice.

To: listenerfeedback@pg2radio.com

From: ameliamyers@wmail.com

Date: March 28

Subject: About Author's Corner

I have been a regular listener to PG2 Radio since thirty years ago, when I was in college. Author's Corner has been my favorite program. I love reading, and listening to authors talk about their works is always fascinating.

Yesterday's program had special meaning to me. I have been a big fan of Hazel Tryniski since I was a child. I love the imaginary worlds she created. Although she is no longer with us now, listening to her son talking about her novels is still very interesting.

Thanks a lot for your great program.

Amelia Myers

186. Who is Carson Tryniski?

    (A) Hazel Tryniski's husband

    (B) Hazel Tryniski's son

    (C) The host of Author's Corner

    (D) The author of *A Happy Rabbit*

187. Why is not Hazel Tryniski on the radio program?

    (A) She is too busy.

    (B) She is currently abroad.

    (C) Her son doesn't allow him.

    (D) She has passed away.

188. If you are interested in basketball, what time should you tune in to PG2 Radio on March 27?

    (A) 18:00

    (B) 19:00

    (C) 20:00

    (D) 21:00

189. What is most likely true about the imaginary worlds Ms. Myers loves?

    (A) The worlds are ruled by magicians.

    (B) The worlds are full of bakeries.

    (C) There animals can talk and think.

    (D) There adults make funny remarks.

190. What is the likely age of Ms. Myers?

    (A) In her teens

    (B) In her early 20s

    (C) In her early 40s

    (D) In her early 50s

GO ON TO THE NEXT PAGE

Backstrong Backpacks
Bikeback Line

Size	Price	Available Colors
20 L	$29.99	Blue, Green, Red, Yellow
30 L	$33.99	Red, Yellow, Black
40 L	$38.99	Blue, Yellow, Black, Pink
50 L	$42.99	Yellow, Black, Orange

Details:

* One large compartment

* Straps to secure a laptop computer in the large compartment

* One smaller compartment to put small items with pockets for pens, keys, glasses, etc.

* One bottom compartment

* Two straps to take stress off your back

* Two side pockets for water bottles or umbrellas

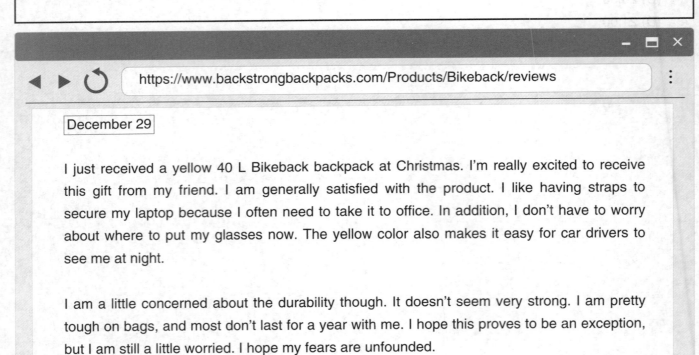

https://www.backstrongbackpacks.com/Products/Bikeback/reviews

December 29

I just received a yellow 40 L Bikeback backpack at Christmas. I'm really excited to receive this gift from my friend. I am generally satisfied with the product. I like having straps to secure my laptop because I often need to take it to office. In addition, I don't have to worry about where to put my glasses now. The yellow color also makes it easy for car drivers to see me at night.

I am a little concerned about the durability though. It doesn't seem very strong. I am pretty tough on bags, and most don't last for a year with me. I hope this proves to be an exception, but I am still a little worried. I hope my fears are unfounded.

Charlie Fisher

https://www.backstrongbackpacks.com/Products/Bikeback/replies

January 2

Dear Mr. Fisher,

Thank you for your feedback regarding your Christmas gift. We understand your concern about the durability. It is a very lightweight backpack. This is due to the use of the newest lightweight materials in the industry. However, it is truly strong and durable. It has survived severe abuse in real life situations during testing.

Every Bikeback backpack comes with a year's warranty. If there are any other problems, please contact us.

Marie Olson
Backstrong Backpacks Customer Service

191. How many sizes does the Bikeback Line offer?
(A) 2
(B) 4
(C) 6
(D) 14

192. How did Mr. Fisher acquire his backpack?
(A) As a Christmas gift
(B) As a birthday present
(C) In a lottery
(D) As a reward

193. What does Mr. Fisher mean when he writes, "I don't have to worry about where to put my glasses now"?
(A) He can put his glasses in the backpack's large compartment.
(B) He can secure his glasses with the backpack's straps.
(C) He can put his glasses in the backpack's side pockets.
(D) He can put his glasses in the backpack's smaller compartment.

194. How much does Mr. Fisher's backpack cost?
(A) $29.99
(B) $33.99
(C) $38.99
(D) $42.99

195. What assurance does Ms. Olson give to Mr. Fisher?
(A) The company will give him a new backpack.
(B) The backpack has one year's warranty.
(C) These backpacks will be available for a long time.
(D) The yellow color is the most popular choice.

GO ON TO THE NEXT PAGE

To: Ruby Brown

From: Sharon Smith

Date: December 18

Subject: Group photo

Dear Mr. Brown,

This is to confirm the photography session at your company next Monday morning. This session should take around 30 minutes. We will shoot at the front gate of your company, and several shots will be taken. As you requested, the entire staff will be photographed together before each department shot is taken.

If you have any questions, please let me know soon. See you on Monday.

Regards,

Sharon Smith

Venus Photo Studio

Attention, all employees! I have exciting news for you. We are to be recognized as the best enterprise in the city for this year. It is the first time our company receives this honor. It is also a testament to the hard work by all of the staff.

We will take a group photo at 9:30 next Monday morning. All the staff will be included in the photo. It will be taken at the main entrance of our building, with our large corporate logo behind everyone.

Please be ready at 9:30 on Monday morning, so we can have the photos taken as quickly as possible.

It has recently been announced that Lincoln Great Spirit Corporation has won the city's Best Enterprise of the Year award. This company, which celebrated its 50th anniversary last year, has been awarded this honor for the first time.

"When I came here six years ago, there were many problems here," said Mr. Graham, the president of the company, "but with the hard work of our staff and the support of our clients, we have been able to completely turn this enterprise around."

"Mr. Graham completely turned things around with his boundless energy and innovative ideas about making progress," said Ruby Brown, a manager at the company.

196. Whom did Ms. Smith write to?

(A) A designer

(B) A journalist

(C) A company's manager

(D) A company's president

197. When will the photography session probably end?

(A) At 9:00

(B) At 10:00

(C) At 11:00

(D) At 12:00

198. What will be in the background of the group photo?

(A) The lawn in front of the building's entrance

(B) The medal of Best Enterprise of the Year

(C) The logo of the company

(D) The poster of a movie star

199. How long has Mr. Graham been at the company?

(A) Six years

(B) Eight years

(C) Ten years

(D) Fifty years

200. What is suggested about Lincoln Great Spirit Corporation?

(A) The employees usually start to work at 9 a.m.

(B) It has won awards many times.

(C) It made a big profit this year.

(D) It is more than fifty years old.

Stop! This is the end of the test. If you finish before time is called, you may go back to Parts 5, 6, and 7 and check your work.

新多益黃金互動 16 週：進階篇模擬試題解答表

Listening Test

題號	答案	題號	答案	題號	答案	題號	答案	題號	答案
1	C	21	C	41	B	61	C	81	C
2	A	22	C	42	A	62	A	82	B
3	B	23	A	43	C	63	C	83	A
4	C	24	B	44	B	64	B	84	D
5	C	25	B	45	D	65	C	85	D
6	D	26	A	46	B	66	B	86	C
7	A	27	B	47	B	67	A	87	D
8	B	28	C	48	C	68	D	88	A
9	A	29	C	49	A	69	B	89	B
10	C	30	B	50	D	70	D	90	C
11	B	31	C	51	B	71	B	91	D
12	A	32	B	52	C	72	A	92	B
13	C	33	A	53	C	73	D	93	C
14	A	34	D	54	B	74	D	94	A
15	B	35	B	55	D	75	C	95	C
16	C	36	D	56	B	76	C	96	D
17	A	37	C	57	A	77	B	97	B
18	C	38	C	58	D	78	C	98	D
19	C	39	B	59	B	79	A	99	A
20	B	40	D	60	D	80	B	100	C

Reading Test

題號	答案	題號	答案	題號	答案	題號	答案	題號	答案
101	C	121	D	141	A	161	B	181	B
102	A	122	B	142	B	162	A	182	D
103	B	123	A	143	C	163	D	183	C
104	D	124	C	144	D	164	B	184	A
105	B	125	C	145	A	165	C	185	B
106	C	126	D	146	B	166	C	186	B
107	A	127	B	147	A	167	B	187	D
108	B	128	A	148	D	168	B	188	A
109	D	129	C	149	C	169	C	189	C
110	A	130	B	150	B	170	B	190	D
111	C	131	B	151	C	171	C	191	B
112	B	132	C	152	B	172	B	192	A
113	B	133	D	153	B	173	D	193	D
114	C	134	A	154	D	174	A	194	C
115	D	135	C	155	A	175	C	195	B
116	B	136	A	156	C	176	C	196	C
117	C	137	B	157	B	177	B	197	B
118	A	138	C	158	C	178	A	198	C
119	B	139	C	159	D	179	D	199	A
120	D	140	B	160	B	180	D	200	D

解析
Listening Test 🎧
聽力測驗

PART 1

C 1. Look at the picture marked number 1 in your test book.

(A) The woman is washing the equipment.

(B) The man is putting on a laboratory coat.

(C) The technicians are conducting experiments in the laboratory.

(D) The professor is typing on a computer.

請看試題本上標號第 1 題的照片。

(A) 女子正在清洗設備。

(B) 男子正穿上實驗衣。

(C) 技術員正在實驗室裡做實驗。

(D) 教授正用電腦打字。

▶說明 照片中的兩人正在實驗室裡專注地進行實驗,故答案為 (C)。

A 2. Look at the picture marked number 2 in your test book.

(A) The building is under construction.

(B) The workers are entering the construction site.

(C) There are two trucks by the crane.

(D) The parking lot is filled with trucks.

請看試題本上標號第 2 題的照片。

(A) 建築物正在興建中。

(B) 工人們正進入工地。

(C) 起重機旁有兩輛卡車。

(D) 停車場停滿貨車。

▶說明 照片中是一棟正在興建而尚未完成的建築物,故答案為 (A)。

B 3. Look at the picture marked number 3 in your test book.

(A) There are some invoices.

(B) There are a lot of coupons.

(C) There are a lot of books.

(D) There are some magazines.

請看試題本上標號第 3 題的照片。

(A) 有一些發票。　　**(B) 有很多折價券。**

(C) 有很多書。　　　(D) 有一些雜誌。

▶說明 照片中陳列一堆顯示各種折扣的折價券,故答案為 (B)。

C 4. Look at the picture marked number 4 in your test book.

(A) People are cleaning the beach.

(B) People are visiting a cultural heritage site.

(C) People are walking on the street.

(D) Some vehicles are driving through a rural landscape.

請看試題本上標號第 4 題的照片。

(A) 人們正在淨灘。

(B) 人們正在參觀文化遺址。

(C) 人們正在街上行走。

(D) 一些車輛駛過鄉村景致。

▶說明 照片中有很多人在一個熱鬧繁華的街道上行走,故答案為 (C)。

C 5. Look at the picture marked number 5 in your test book.

(A) The car is in a repair shop.

(B) The workers are sitting on the floor.

(C) The equipment is operating in a factory.

(D) The man is passing a writing board to his colleague.

請看試題本上標號第 5 題的照片。

(A) 車子在修車店。

(B) 工人坐在地板上。

(C) 設備在工廠運作中。

(D) 男子正把寫字板傳給同事。

▶說明 照片中有兩名工人正在監控運作中的機器,故答案為 (C)。

D 6. Look at the picture marked number 6 in your test book.

(A) They are reading at a library.

(B) They are feasting at a banquet.

(C) They are watching a movie.

(D) They are attending a conference.

(A) 他們正在圖書館看書。

(B) 他們正在宴會上享用大餐。

(C) 他們正在看電影。

(D) 他們正在參加會議。

▶說明 照片中的人們正在進行一場大型會議，故答案為 (D)。

PART 2

A 7. Would you translate this letter into French for me?

(A) Sure, let me see it.

(B) I don't have it.

(C) There are thirty minutes left.

你能幫我將這封信翻成法文嗎？

(A) 當然，讓我看一下。

(B) 我沒有這封信。

(C) 還剩下三十分鐘。

▶說明 題目詢問對方願不願意翻譯信件，故 (A) 的肯定答覆是合理的回應。

B 8. How many tickets did you buy?

(A) For the movie.

(B) Four.

(C) I'll be there soon.

你買了幾張票？

(A) 為了這部電影。

(B) 四張。

(C) 我很快就會到達那裡。

▶說明 題目詢問對方買了幾張票，故 (B) 回答數字四張是正確答案。

A 9. Where can I buy a cup of tea?

(A) At the tea shop on the corner.

(B) Any time after 10 a.m.

(C) I prefer coffee.

我在哪裡可以買到茶飲？

(A) 轉角那家茶飲店。

(B) 早上十點過後都可以。

(C) 我偏好咖啡。

▶說明 題目詢問對方在何處可以買到茶，故 (A) 回答明確的地點是正確答案。

C 10. Why did you come to the office so early today?

(A) At 8:00 this morning.

(B) I overslept.

(C) The bus was earlier than usual.

為何你今天這麼早來辦公室？

(A) 今天早上八點鐘。

(B) 我睡過頭了。

(C) 公車比平時早到。

▶說明 題目詢問對方今天提早到辦公室的原因，故 (C) 解釋因為公車提早到是合理的回應。

B 11. Have you opened the door to the office?

(A) No problem.

(B) Actually I forgot to bring the key.

(C) I don't like our office building.

你打開辦公室的門了嗎？

(A) 沒問題。

(B) 其實我忘了帶鑰匙。

(C) 我不喜歡我們的辦公大樓。

▶說明 題目詢問對方是否已打開辦公室的門，故 (B) 暗示因為沒帶鑰匙所以還沒開門是合理的回應。

A 12. You went to the baseball game last weekend, didn't you?

(A) I was too busy to go.

(B) I bumped into an old friend last Sunday.

(C) A few hours ago.

你上週末去看了棒球賽，對吧？

(A) 我太忙了而無法去。

(B) 我上週日與一位老朋友不期而遇。

(C) 幾個小時之前。

▶說明 題目詢問對方上週末是否去看了

棒球賽，故 (A) 答覆因太忙而沒有去是合理的回應。

C 13. How many students will join the summer camp?

(A) We need to advertise for a new teacher.

(B) They will arrive in early July.

(C) About one hundred and twenty.

有多少學生會參加夏令營？

(A) 我們需要登廣告來招募一位新老師。

(B) 他們在七月初會抵達。

(C) 大約一百二十位。

▶說明 題目詢問對方共有多少學生會參加夏令營，故 (C) 回答人數是正確答案。

A 14. When will you work on Tuesday?

(A) I'll be on the night shift.

(B) Six hours.

(C) See you tomorrow.

你星期二是何時上班？

(A) 我會上夜班。

(B) 六個小時。

(C) 明天見。

▶說明 題目詢問對方星期二何時上班，故 (A) 回答上夜班是合理的回應。

B 15. We're going out for lunch on Friday.

(A) I'm not hungry.

(B) Sorry, I can't make it.

(C) The beef noodles were delicious.

我們星期五會去外面吃午餐。

(A) 我不餓。

(B) 抱歉，我無法參加。

(C) 牛肉麵很美味。

▶說明 題目是藉由跟對方說星期五中午會外出用餐來進行邀約，故 (B) 回答無法參加是合理的回應。

C 16. When does the flight to Tokyo leave?

(A) At Gate 17.

(B) Because of bad weather.

(C) Thirty minutes behind schedule.

前往東京的班機何時起飛？

(A) 在十七號登機門。

(B) 因為天候不佳。

(C) 比預定時間晚三十分鐘。

▶說明 題目詢問對方飛往東京的班機何時起飛，故 (C) 回答比預訂時間延遲三十分鐘是正確答案。

A 17. How will I know if the marathon is canceled?

(A) It'll be announced on TV.

(B) It won't be tomorrow.

(C) It'll be held in the suburbs.

我會如何得知馬拉松是否被取消？

(A) 會在電視上宣布。

(B) 不會是明天。

(C) 會在郊區舉辦。

▶說明 題目詢問對方如何得知馬拉松是否取消，故 (A) 回答可以從電視上得知是合理的回應。

C 18. Why not make some changes to our plan?

(A) Keep the change.

(B) Because Charlie won't come.

(C) That's a good idea.

何不調整一下我們的計畫呢？

(A) 零錢不用找。

(B) 因為 Charlie 不會來。

(C) 好主意。

▶說明 題目建議對方在計畫上做一些調整，故 (C) 贊成這個建議是合理的回應。

C 19. Did you create a chart to track your income for the year?

(A) They charged me $80.

(B) I paid income tax last month.

(C) Yeah, I just did it.

你做了圖表來記錄你今年的收入嗎？

(A) 他們收我八十美元。

(B) 我上個月繳了所得稅。

(C) 是的，我剛做了。

▶說明 題目詢問對方是否製作了圖表來記錄今年的收入，故 (C) 肯定答覆自己剛剛做了是合理的回應。

B 20. Where can I donate these books?

(A) On the table.

(B) What kind of books are they?

(C) I like reading books.

我可以把這些書捐到何處？

(A) 在桌上。

(B) 它們是哪一類的書？

(C) 我喜歡閱讀書籍。

▶說明 題目詢問對方何處可以捐贈書籍，故 (B) 想進一步了解並反問對方是哪類書籍是合理的回應。

C 21. I'll lose my registration fee if I can't make it, right?

(A) Check the lost-and-found.

(B) It's in the desk drawer.

(C) I'm afraid you will.

如果我無法趕上，就會損失報名費，對吧？

(A) 去失物招領處看一下。

(B) 它在書桌抽屜裡。

(C) 恐怕是的。

▶說明 題目想跟對方確認如果沒趕上是否會損失報名費，故 (C) 的肯定答覆是合理的回應。

C 22. Did Miranda win the scholarship?

(A) She went to college in Australia.

(B) Yes, I'm looking forward to it.

(C) She'll tell us about it tomorrow.

Miranda 獲得了獎學金嗎？

(A) 她在澳洲上大學。

(B) 是的，我很期待這件事。

(C) 她明天會跟我們說這件事。

▶說明 題目詢問對方 Miranda 是否拿到了獎學金，故 (C) 回答 Miranda 明天會自己宣布是合理的回應。

A 23. The MRT line is still being built.

(A) It won't be finished until next year.

(B) The construction will soon begin.

(C) No, it's under the road.

這條捷運路線仍然在興建中。

(A) 它要到明年才會完工。

(B) 興建工程很快會開始。

(C) 不對，它是在馬路底下。

▶說明 題目告訴對方某條捷運線仍在施工中，故 (A) 說要到明年才會完工是合理的回應。

B 24. Have we changed our tea supplier?

(A) The tea is of good quality.

(B) I have no idea.

(C) It's on the shelf over there.

我們更換了茶葉供應商嗎？

(A) 這種茶的品質很好。

(B) 我不知道。

(C) 它在那邊的架子上。

▶說明 題目詢問對方是否更換了茶葉供應商，故 (B) 回答不太清楚是合理的回應。

B 25. What's on exhibit at the science museum?

(A) It opens at 8:30 a.m.

(B) Dinosaur fossils.

(C) The children are very excited.

科學博物館目前展出什麼？

(A) 它早上八點三十分開門。

(B) 恐龍化石。

(C) 孩子們非常興奮。

▶說明 題目詢問對方科博館目前的展出內容，故 (B) 回答展出恐龍化石為合理的回應。

A 26. Shall we go shopping or go to the movies tonight?

(A) We have time to do both.

(B) There's no time next week.

(C) I don't like that restaurant.

我們今晚要去逛街還是去看電影？

(A) 我們有時間去做這兩件事。

(B) 下週沒有時間。

(C) 我不喜歡那家餐廳。

說明 題目詢問對方今晚的行程是去逛街購物還是看電影,故 (A) 回答兩件事都可以做是合理的回應。

B 27. Do you take this bus to work?

(A) It passes my place.

(B) I go to work by train.

(C) It usually leaves at 7:00 a.m.

你是搭這班公車去上班的嗎?

(A) 它經過我家。

(B) 我搭火車上班。

(C) 它通常在早上七點離站。

說明 題目詢問對方是否搭某班公車去上班,(B) 回答是搭火車上班,表示並非搭公車,是合理的回應。

C 28. Have you heard about the news that Jeremy will be promoted?

(A) You've been in the news.

(B) I'll go to his wedding.

(C) I didn't know that.

你有聽說 Jeremy 要升職的消息嗎?

(A) 你上新聞了。

(B) 我會去參加他的婚禮。

(C) 我沒聽說。

說明 題目詢問對方是否聽說 Jeremy 要升職的消息,故 (C) 回答不知道這個消息是合理的回應。

C 29. You'd better call Mr. Clark to confirm the booking.

(A) He won't agree with me.

(B) But it is fully booked.

(C) I called, but he didn't answer.

你最好打電話給 Clark 先生確認這項預訂。

(A) 他不會同意我的。

(B) 但已經訂滿了。

(C) 我打了,但他沒有接。

說明 題目建議對方打電話確認預訂,故 (C) 回答已經打了但 Clark 先生沒有接電話是合理的回應。

B 30. I don't know which model of car to choose.

(A) These models are very slim.

(B) Which model can you afford?

(C) I can give you a ride.

我不知道該選哪種型號的車。

(A) 這些模特兒非常苗條。

(B) 你負擔得起哪種型號?

(C) 我可以載你一程。

說明 題目詢問對方的建議,表達自己不知該買哪一款車,故 (B) 反問其能負擔得起哪款車是合理的回應。

C 31. Where did you see that movie review?

(A) I like it very much.

(B) It was a box-office success.

(C) In the newspaper.

你在哪裡看到那篇影評?

(A) 我非常喜歡它。

(B) 它非常賣座。

(C) 在報紙上。

說明 題目詢問對方在何處看到影評,故 (C) 回答在報紙上是合理的回應。

PART 3

Questions 32–34 refer to the following conversation.

M: This is a really cool pink shirt. Do you have any in small?

W: I'm afraid we don't have any in small size. Maybe you can try the medium one.

M: Medium doesn't fit me very well. It's too big.

W: Well, we have some of the same style in blue over here. They are available in different sizes. Will these be OK?

請參考以下的對話回答**第 32 題至 34 題**。

男:這是一件非常有型的粉色襯衫。你們這件襯衫有小號的嗎?

女:恐怕我們沒有小號的了。或許您可以試看看中號的。

男:我穿中號不太合身。太大了。

女：嗯，我們這邊有一些相同款式的藍色襯衫。它們各種尺碼都有。這些可以嗎？

B 32. Where does this conversation most likely take place?

(A) In a record store

(B) In a clothing store

(C) In a convenience store

(D) In a dry cleaner's

此對話最有可能發生的地點是哪裡？

(A) 在唱片行　　　**(B) 在服裝店**

(C) 在便利商店　　(D) 在乾洗店

▶說明 對話一開始男子在詢問對方關於襯衫的尺寸問題，可知答案為 (B)。

A 33. What is the problem?

(A) The pink shirt is too big for the man.

(B) The man wants to return the record.

(C) The beverages all sold out.

(D) The man can't find his shirt.

問題是什麼？

(A) 粉色襯衫對男子來說太大了。

(B) 男子想要退掉唱片。

(C) 飲料全部售完。

(D) 男子找不到他的襯衫。

▶說明 從對話中男子反應 "Medium doesn't fit me very well. It's too big."，可知粉色中號襯衫對他來說太大、不合身，故選 (A)。

D 34. What does the woman suggest the man do?

(A) Go to another store

(B) Buy the shirt of medium size

(C) Call the customer service

(D) Choose a different color

女子建議男子做什麼？

(A) 去另一家店

(B) 購買中號的襯衫

(C) 打電話到客服部

(D) 選擇另一個顏色

▶說明 從對話最後女子回應他們有一些

相同款式的藍色襯衫且有不同尺寸，可知答案為 (D)。

Questions 35–37 refer to the following conversation.

W: Sorry. I want to work out today, but I just found that I forgot my membership card at home.

M: No problem. If you have any identification with you, I can look up your membership in the computer.

W: Well, I have my driver's license. My name and address are right here.

M: OK. Wait a moment, please. I see your information here. Your membership will expire in the end of the year. Here is a one-day pass, but you won't be able to use it tomorrow.

請參考以下的對話回答**第 35 題至 37 題**。

女：不好意思。我今天想要運動，但我剛發現我把會員卡忘在家裡了。

男：沒問題。如果你身上有任何身分證明文件，我可以從電腦查詢你的會員身分。

女：嗯，我有駕照。我的名字和地址在這邊。

男：好的。請稍候。我在這裡看到你的資料了。你的會員身分將會在今年年底過期。這是一日通行證，不過你明天就無法使用這張了。

B 35. What does the woman want to do?

(A) Apply for membership of the gym

(B) Work out in the gym

(C) Ask the man out

(D) Drive a car

女子想要做什麼？

(A) 申請這家健身房的會員資格

(B) 在健身房運動

(C) 邀約男子

(D) 開車

▶說明 從對話第一句女子就明確表示她想要運動健身，可知答案為 (B)。

D 36. Who is most likely the man?

(A) A security guard

(B) A trainer

(C) A member of the gym

(D) An employee of the gym

男子最有可能是什麼身分？

(A) 警衛　　　　　(B) 教練

(C) 健身房的會員　**(D) 健身房的員工**

▶說明 從對話中男子要求女子提供身份證明以便查詢其會員身分，可推知男子為健身房的員工，故選 (D)。

C 37. What does the man give the woman?

(A) A new membership card

(B) An identity card

(C) A pass to use for today only

(D) His phone number

男子給女子什麼東西？

(A) 新的會員卡

(B) 身分證

(C) 只限今天使用的通行證

(D) 他的電話號碼

▶說明 從對話最後一句 "Here is a one-day pass"，可知男子給女子一張一日通行證，故選 (C)。

Questions 38–40 refer to the following conversation.

M: Good morning. Super Wise GPS Equipment. This is the customer service department. How may I help you?

W: Hello. My friend gave me his Super Wise Runner A–5 Model. He lost its instruction manual, so I don't know how to use it.

M: That is our earlier model. We no longer produce it.

W: Is that a problem?

M: I don't think so. Give me a moment to check. It's good news that its instruction manual is still on our website.

W: Could you send me the link to the manual? I can't find your website.

M: Sure. Please give me your e-mail address.

I can send you the link immediately.

請參考以下的對話回答**第 38 題至 40 題**。

男：早安，Super Wise 全球衛星定位系統設備。這裡是客服部。我可以如何協助您？

女：你好。我的朋友給了我他的 Super Wise Runner A–5 型號。他弄丟了操作指南，所以我不知道如何使用它。

男：那是我們比較早期的型號。我們沒有再生產了。

女：那是個問題嗎？

男：我不認為如此。給我一點時間查一下。好消息是它的操作指南仍然放在我們的網站上。

女：你能傳給我指南的連結嗎？我找不到你們的網站。

男：當然。請給我您的電子郵件地址。我可以馬上將連結傳給您。

C 38. What is true about the Runner A–5 Model?

(A) It is the latest model.

(B) The woman wants to buy it.

(C) The company has stopped producing it.

(D) The man can't find its manual.

關於 Runner A–5 型號，何者為真？

(A) 它是最新的型號。

(B) 女子想要買它。

(C) 公司已經停止生產它。

(D) 男子找不到它的使用指南。

▶說明 從對話中男子提到 "We no longer produce it."，可知 Runner A–5 型號已經停產，故選 (C)。

B 39. What does the woman request?

(A) A catalog　　**(B) A link**

(C) A new model　(D) An address

女子要求什麼東西？

(A) 商品型錄　　**(B) 網路連結**

(C) 新的型號　　(D) 地址

▶說明 從對話中女子提到 "Could you send me a link to the manual?"，可知她

要求對方給她操作指南的連結，故選
(B)。

D 40. What will the woman most likely do next?

(A) Go to the store with her friend

(B) Select a new GPS model

(C) Check out her bank account

(D) Tell the man her e-mail address

女子接下來最可能做什麼？

(A) 和朋友去那一家店

(B) 挑選一個新的 GPS 型號

(C) 查看自己的銀行帳戶

(D) 告訴男子她的電子郵件地址

▶說明 從對話最後男子要女子提供電子郵件以便將連結傳送給她，可推知答案為 (D)。

Questions 41–43 refer to the following conversation with three speakers.

M: Did you know that the baseball tournament will start this weekend?

W1: I heard someone mentioning it.

W2: It should be a big sports event. Are any good teams coming to play?

M: Japan, South Korea, Cuba and the Netherlands are all coming to play.

W1: Isn't it too late to get the tickets?

M: Probably for the Taiwan games, but there are still tickets available for the other games.

W2: Are there any games this Sunday afternoon?

M: Japan versus South Korea at 2:30 p.m.

W2: That should be a great game.

M: No doubt about it! Maybe we can watch it together.

請參考以下的三人對話回答**第 41 題至 43 題**。

男：你知道棒球錦標賽這個週末要開打了嗎？

女 1：我聽到別人提起過這件事。

女 2：這應該是大型的運動賽事。有任何不錯的球隊來參賽嗎？

男：日本、南韓、古巴和荷蘭都會來參賽。

女 1：現在是不是太晚，買不到票了？

男：對有臺灣出賽的比賽來說或許是，但是其他比賽的場次仍然有票可以買。

女 2：這個星期日下午有任何比賽嗎？

男：下午兩點半有一場日本對南韓的比賽。

女 2：那應該是一場精彩的比賽。

男：那毋庸置疑！或許我們可以一起去看。

B 41. What is the conversation mainly about?

(A) How to play baseball

(B) A baseball tournament

(C) Taiwan's baseball teams

(D) The speakers' favorite sports

對話主要是關於什麼？

(A) 如何打棒球

(B) 棒球錦標賽

(C) 臺灣的棒球隊

(D) 說話者最喜愛的運動

▶說明 從對話一開始男子詢問女子們是否知道棒球錦標賽這個週末要開打這件事，可知對話重點在討論棒球錦標賽，故選 (B)。

A 42. Why does the man say, "No doubt about it"?

(A) He thinks the game must be great.

(B) He believes Japan is more likely to win.

(C) He is certain about the game time.

(D) He strongly disagrees with the women.

為什麼男子說「那毋庸置疑」？

(A) 他認為比賽一定很精彩。

(B) 他相信日本勝算較大。

(C) 他很確定比賽時間。

(D) 他非常不同意女子們的想法。

▶說明 對話最後，其中一位女子表示日本對南韓的那場比賽應該很精彩，接著男子回應 "No doubt about it"，故選 (A)。

C 43. What does the man suggest?

(A) Buying tickets to tomorrow's game

(B) Talking about basketball

(C) Watching a game together

(D) Playing baseball this afternoon

男子建議做什麼？

(A) 買明天比賽的票

(B) 聊聊籃球

(C) 一起看比賽

(D) 下午打棒球

▶說明 對話最後男子提到 "Maybe we can watch it together"，故選 (C)。

Questions 44–46 refer to the following conversation.

W: Hello. I'm Patty Jones. I have just opened a new travel agency and need to find effective ways to advertise it. My friend told me that your company designed a website for his restaurant and advised me to give you a call.

M: Thank you for calling, Ms. Jones. We have experienced web consultants who can help you design a suitable website to make your travel agency stand out from the others.

W: That sounds wonderful. Could I make an appointment to talk with one of your consultants next week?

M: Certainly. Before I transfer your call, would you mind telling me who your friend is? We'd like to know who recommended our services.

請參考以下的對話回答**第 44 題至 46 題**。

女：你好，我是 Patty Jones。我剛開了一間新的旅行社，需要找到有效的方法宣傳它。我的朋友告訴我說你們公司幫他的餐廳設計了網站，並建議我打電話給你們。

男：Jones 小姐，感謝您的來電。我們有經驗豐富的網路顧問可以幫助您設計適合的網站，讓您的旅行社出類拔萃。

女：那聽起來很棒。我能否預約下週去和你們

的顧問商談？

男：當然可以。在我為您轉接電話前，可否告訴我您的朋友是誰？我們想知道是誰推薦了我們的服務。

B 44. What kind of service is provided by the man's company?

(A) Travel arrangements

(B) Web design

(C) Restaurant decoration

(D) Financial investment

男子的公司提供哪一類的服務？

(A) 旅遊籌劃　　　　**(B) 網頁設計**

(C) 餐廳裝潢　　　　(D) 財務投資

▶說明 從對話一開始女子提到她是經由朋友推薦而得知男子的公司能為客戶設計網站，故選 (B)。

D 45. When is the woman's appointment?

(A) Tomorrow　　　(B) This Friday

(C) This weekend　**(D) Next week**

女子預約會面的時間是何時？

(A) 明天　　　　　(B) 這週五

(C) 這週末　　　　**(D) 下星期**

▶說明 從對話中女子提到 "Could I make an appointment . . . next week?"，而男子回答沒問題，可知她跟顧問見面的時間約在下星期，故選 (D)。

B 46. What information is the woman asked to provide?

(A) When she is available

(B) Who recommended the services

(C) How much her budget is

(D) What she plans to do

女子被要求提供什麼資訊？

(A) 她何時有空

(B) 誰推薦這個服務

(C) 她的預算是多少

(D) 她計畫要做什麼

▶說明 從對話最後男子詢問 ". . . would you mind telling me who your friend is? We'd like to know who recommended

our services."，可知他要女子告訴他推薦
人是誰，故選 (B)。

Questions 47–49 refer to the following conversation.

M: Hello, my name is Jerry Adams. I am in Boston for the summer to explore the city. I'm wondering if you need any summer help, so I could earn some money to support myself.

W: Well, we are very busy now because it's the baseball season. Do you have any experience working in restaurants?

M: I've worked in the kitchen at a couple of restaurants in San Francisco. I have the information here on my résumé. I also have two former employers who can give my references.

W: It sounds good. Our head chef is in the office. I can introduce you to him now.

請參考以下的對話回答**第 47 題至 49 題**。

男：你好，我的名字叫 Jerry Adams。我這個夏天會在波士頓探訪這個城市。我在想你們是否需要任何夏日的助手，這樣我可以賺點錢來供養自己。

女：嗯，我們現在很忙，因為棒球季的關係。你有任何在餐廳工作的經驗嗎？

男：我在舊金山的一些餐廳的廚房工作過。我的履歷表這裡有這些資料。我也有兩名前任雇主可以幫我寫推薦信。

女：聽起來不錯。我們的首席廚師正在辦公室裡。我現在可以將你介紹給他。

B 47. What city are the speakers in now?

(A) San Francisco **(B) Boston**
(C) Houston (D) San Diego

說話者現在正在哪個城市？
(A) 舊金山 **(B) 波士頓**
(C) 休士頓 (D) 聖地牙哥
▶說明 從對話一開頭男子提到他正在波士頓探訪這個城市，可知答案為 (B)。

C 48. Why is the restaurant busy now?

(A) It just moved to the downtown area.
(B) It has become very famous.
(C) The baseball season has begun.
(D) Many tourists have their holidays there.

餐廳現在為何很忙碌？
(A) 它剛搬到市中心。
(B) 它已經變得很有名。
(C) 棒球季已經開始。
(D) 許多遊客在那裡度假。
▶說明 對話中女子提到 "we are very busy now because it's the baseball season"，可知是因為棒球季的關係，故選 (C)。

A 49. Who will the man probably speak with next?

(A) The head chef
(B) A customer in the restaurant
(C) The hiring manager
(D) The owner of the restaurant

男子接下來可能會和誰談話？
(A) 首席廚師
(B) 餐廳裡的一名客人
(C) 招聘經理
(D) 餐廳老闆
▶說明 對話最後女子提到 "Our head chef is in the office. I can introduce you to him now."，可知男子將和餐廳的首席廚師談話，故選 (A)。

Questions 50–52 refer to the following conversation.

W: Hello, Gilbert. We just got a call from the Nelson Company. They want to know when we can start work on their new plant in Surrey. Do you have any idea when the construction work will begin?

M: There is a problem. Some of the local residents have talked with the government, and they are delaying any work we can do. We need to meet with the city planners next week. I think the Nelson Company officials should accompany us to the meeting.

W: Shall I call them back and inform them of this?

M: Yes, that would be great.

W: When is the meeting?

M: It will be held at City Hall at 7:30 p.m. next Tuesday.

請參考以下的對話回答**第 50 題至 52 題**。

女：你好，Gilbert。我們剛接到 Nelson 公司的來電。他們想要知道我們何時可以進行他們在薩里的新工廠工程。你知道營造工作何時會動工嗎？

男：有一個問題。當地的一些居民和政府溝通過了，並且在延誤任何我們能做的工作。我們下週需要和城市規畫人員會面。我認為 Nelson 公司的要員應該陪同我們去參加這個會議。

女：我要回電告知他們這件事嗎？

男：好的，那太好了。

女：會議是什麼時候？

男：在下週二晚上七點三十分在市政廳舉行。

D 50. What do the speakers most likely work for?

(A) A plant

(B) The government

(C) The Nelson Company

(D) A construction company

說話者最有可能在哪裡工作？

(A) 工廠　　　　(B) 政府

(C) Nelson 公司　**(D) 建設公司**

▶說明 對話開頭女子提到 Nelson 公司想要知道何時可以進行他們在薩里的新工廠工程，故可推測這兩名說話者是在建設公司工作，故選 (D)。

B 51. Why has the construction work not begun?

(A) The site is not safe.

(B) The residents are delaying it.

(C) The Nelson Company is short of funds.

(D) The Nelson Company has changed their plan.

為何營造工程還沒開始？

(A) 地點不安全。

(B) 居民延誤了工程。

(C) Nelson 公司的資金短缺。

(D) Nelson 公司改變了他們的計畫。

▶說明 對話中男子提到 "Some of the local residents . . . delaying any work we can do."，可知是因為當地居民延誤工程開工，故選 (B)。

C 52. When will the meeting take place?

(A) At 7:30 a.m. this Tuesday

(B) At 7:30 this evening

(C) At 7:30 p.m. next Tuesday

(D) At 7:30 a.m. next Thursday

會議何時會舉行？

(A) 本週二早上七點三十分

(B) 今天晚上七點三十分

(C) 下週二晚上七點三十分

(D) 下週四晚上七點三十分

▶說明 對話最後男子提到會議舉行的時間 "The meeting will be held at City Hall at 7:30 p.m. next Tuesday."，故選 (C)。

Questions 53–55 refer to the following conversation.

W: It's hard to believe that the Sydney convention is only four days away.

M: There will be some famous people attending it. Has all of the transportation been arranged?

W: The flight tickets are all confirmed. We will be flying to Sydney out of London Gatwick Airport via Dubai.

M: Has ground transportation been arranged?

W: It's your job! You said you would call the car rental company.

M: Oops! I forgot about it. I'll call them later and also check if there's a shuttle bus from the airport to the hotel we stay in.

請參考以下的對話回答**第 53 題至 55 題**。

女：不敢相信雪梨會議再四天後就要舉行了。

男：將會有一些名人參加。所有的交通都安排了嗎？

女：機票全都確認好了。我們將會從倫敦的蓋威克機場經過杜拜轉機飛往雪梨。

男：地面交通安排了嗎？

女：那是你的工作！你說你會打電話給租車公司。

男：哎呀！我忘了這件事。我稍後會打給他們，也會查詢一下從機場到我們住的飯店是否有接駁車。

C 53. What is the conversation mainly about?
    (A) A vacation in Dubai
    (B) A trip to London
    (C) A convention in Sydney
    (D) A car rental company

對話主要是關於什麼？
(A) 杜拜的假期　　(B) 去倫敦的旅程
(C) 雪梨的會議　　(D) 一家租車公司

▶說明 對話開頭女子就明確提起雪梨會議在四天後就要舉行了，而後的對話內容主要在說為雪梨會議安排各項交通的事情，故選 (C)。

B 54. What is the problem that the speakers find?
    (A) They can't afford the rent.
    (B) No one has arranged ground transportation yet.
    (C) There is no shuttle bus service from the airport to their hotel.
    (D) They forgot to reserve plane tickets.

說話者發現什麼問題？
(A) 他們無法負擔租金。
(B) 還沒有人安排地面交通。
(C) 從機場到他們住的飯店沒有接駁車服務。

(D) 他們忘了預訂機票。

▶說明 對話中男子詢問 "Has ground transportation been arranged?"，而女子回覆男子那是他應該負責的，但男子卻說他忘記了，可推知還沒有人安排地面交通事宜，故選 (B)。

D 55. What will the man most likely do next?
    (A) Cancel the trip
    (B) Book air tickets
    (C) Talk to some famous people
    (D) Call the car rental company

男子接下來最有可能會做什麼？
(A) 取消旅程
(B) 預訂機票
(C) 和一些名人談話
(D) 打電話給租車公司

▶說明 對話最後男子說他稍後會打電話給租車公司，故選 (D)。

Questions 56–58 refer to the following conversation.

W: I need to replace the battery in my digital camera, but I can't find the type mine uses here.

M: Let me see which model of camera you have. Oh, it's an older model. We don't have any of these batteries in stock, but we can order one for you.

W: How long would it take for a battery to arrive?

M: It should be two or three days. If you give me your phone number, I can call you when it arrives.

請參考以下的對話回答**第 56 題至 58 題**。

女：我需要更換我的數位相機的電池，但我在這裡找不到我的相機使用的那種電池。

男：讓我看一下您的相機是哪一種型號。噢，這是比較舊的型號。這種電池我們沒有庫存，但我們可以幫您訂購一顆。

女：電池要多久才會到貨？

男：應該是兩到三天。如果您給我您的電話，到貨時我可以打電話給您。

B 56. What is the woman's problem?

(A) She needs a new digital camera.

(B) She can't find the battery she needs.

(C) The battery she needs is too expensive.

(D) Her camera needs to be fixed.

女子的問題是什麼？

(A) 她需要一臺新的數位相機。

(B) 她找不到她需要的電池。

(C) 她需要的電池太貴了。

(D) 她的相機需要修理。

▶說明 從對話一開始女子就提到她找不到她所需要的數位相機的電池，故選 (B)。

A 57. What does the man say about the woman's digital camera?

(A) It is an older model.

(B) It is out of stock.

(C) It is beyond repair.

(D) It is a valuable antique.

關於女子的數位相機，男子說了什麼？

(A) 它是比較舊的型號。

(B) 它缺貨。

(C) 它無法修理了。

(D) 它是一臺值錢的古董。

▶說明 對話中男子檢視女子的數位相機後評論 "it's an older model."，故選 (A)。

D 58. What will the woman most likely do next?

(A) Go to another store to look for the battery she needs

(B) Get into an argument with the man

(C) Purchase a battery online

(D) Give the man her phone number

女子接下來最可能會做什麼？

(A) 去另一家店尋找她需要的電池

(B) 和男子爭論

(C) 在網路上購買電池

(D) 給男子她的電話號碼

▶說明 對話最後男子向女子索取電話號碼以便電池到貨時通知她來取貨，而女子也表示同意，故選 (D)。

Questions 59–61 refer to the following conversation.

W: We really need to clean our office. Do we have the number for any office cleaners in the area?

M: Let me check the telephone directory. Yes, there is the Shiny Cleaning Company. Their phone number is right here.

W: If I call them now, when should we arrange for them to clean the office?

M: Either Saturday or Sunday would be best. There will be fewer people working then, so it will cause less inconvenience than during the week.

W: OK. I will give them a call right now.

請參考以下的對話回答**第 59 題至 61 題**。

女：我們真的需要清掃我們的辦公室。你有這個區域任何辦公室清潔工的電話嗎？

男：我查一下電話簿。有的，這裡有一家 Shiny 清潔公司。他們的電話就在這裡。

女：如果我現在打給他們，我們應該安排何時讓他們過來打掃辦公室？

男：最好是星期六或星期日。那時比較少人上班，所以會比平日造成較少的不便。

女：好的。我現在就打電話給他們。

B 59. Who are most likely the speakers?

(A) Cleaners   **(B) Office workers**

(C) Sales clerks   (D) Drivers

說話者最可能是誰？

(A) 清潔工   **(B) 辦公室職員**

(C) 店員   (D) 駕駛員

▶說明 根據對話內容，說話者在商量要安排清潔工到辦公室打掃，並在討論哪個時段比較不會影響到同仁工作，故選 (B)。

D 60. When will the cleaning most likely take

place?

(A) Monday or Tuesday

(B) Tuesday or Wednesday

(C) Thursday or Friday

(D) Saturday or Sunday

清潔工作最可能何時進行？

(A) 週一或週二　　(B) 週二或週三

(C) 週四或週五　　**(D) 週六或週日**

▶說明 對話中男子提到 "Either Saturday or Sunday would be best."，故選 (D)。

C 61. What is the woman probably going to do next?

(A) Clean the office

(B) Talk to her boss

(C) Call the cleaning company

(D) Get back to work

女子接下來可能會做什麼？

(A) 清掃辦公室

(B) 和老闆談話

(C) 打電話給清潔公司

(D) 回到工作崗位

▶說明 對話最後女子提到她馬上就會打電話給清潔公司，故選 (C)。

Questions 62–64 refer to the following conversation.

M: I just got another call from a dissatisfied customer. She said that the expiry date on the milk is still three days away, but the milk tastes bad.

W: That is the third such call today. Do you think there might be a problem with the freezer?

M: Were all of the calls about the same brand?

W: No, they were about different brands of milk.

M: Then it might be a freezer problem. I'll call a technician and ask him to take a look at it immediately.

請參考以下的對話回答**第 62 題至 64 題**。

男：我剛才又接到不滿的客人打來的電話。她說牛奶的保存期限還有三天，但是喝起來味道很糟。

女：那是今天第三通這樣的電話了。你覺得問題可能是出在冰櫃嗎？

男：全部的電話都是關於同一個品牌嗎？

女：不是，是關於不同的品牌。

男：那麼就有可能是冰櫃的問題。我會打電話給技師，並請他馬上過來看一下。

A 62. What is the problem?

(A) Customers are complaining about the milk.

(B) The man is taking too many phone calls.

(C) The woman is not satisfied with the milk.

(D) The store is going to close down.

問題是什麼？

(A) 顧客投訴關於牛奶的事。

(B) 男子接到太多電話。

(C) 女子對於牛奶不滿意。

(D) 商店即將要倒閉。

▶說明 對話一開始男子提到他剛才又接到客人打電話來抱怨牛奶，故選 (A)。

C 63. What do the speakers think the cause of the problem may be?

(A) The supplier sends them products of poor quality.

(B) The business is getting worse.

(C) There might be something wrong with the freezer.

(D) Too many colleagues are off today.

男子認為問題的原因可能為何？

(A) 供應商提供品質不佳的產品。

(B) 生意每況愈下。

(C) 冰櫃可能出了問題。

(D) 今天太多同事請假。

▶說明 對話最後男子推測說牛奶壞掉的原因應該和冰櫃有關聯，故選 (C)。

B 64. How will the man solve the problem?

(A) He will use a new way to promote the milk.

(B) He will contact a technician.

(C) He will apologize to the customers.

(D) He will call the HR manager.

男子將會如何解決問題？

(A) 他將會用新方法促銷牛奶。

(B) 他將會連絡技師。

(C) 他將向顧客道歉。

(D) 他將打電話給人資經理。

▶說明 對話最後男子說他會打電話給技師，故選 (B)。

Questions 65–67 refer to the following conversation and table of extra charges.

M: Hello, I am calling to reserve a plane ticket from Boston to Los Angeles. I would like to leave in the morning next Wednesday, before 8 o'clock, if possible.

W: Sure. There is a flight of American Airlines departing at 7:45 a.m. The fare is five hundred and twenty-five dollars, including tax.

M: That sounds fine. Please book me on this one. By the way, would it be possible to take a small pet dog on the flight?

W: Yes, there should be no problem. But you need to pay an extra fee to take the dog aboard.

請參考以下的對話及額外收費表回答**第 65 題至 67 題**。

男：你好，我打電話來是要預訂從波士頓到洛杉磯的機票。我想要在下星期三早上離開，如果可能的話在八點以前。

女：好的。美國航空有一架班機在早上七點四十五分起飛。票價含稅是五百二十五美元。

男：聽起來不錯。請幫我訂這一班。對了，有可能帶小型寵物狗上飛機嗎？

女：可以，那應該沒問題。但你必須付額外費用才能帶狗上飛機。

額外收費
■ 餐點：十五美元
■ 嬰兒手推車 (托運)：十美元
■ 座位選擇：三十美元
■ 小型寵物 (放置籠內)：二十五美元
■ 更改預訂：五十美元

C 65. Where does the woman most likely work?

(A) At a train station

(B) At a pet store

(C) At a travel agency

(D) At a department store

女子最有可能在哪裡上班？

(A) 在火車站 　　(B) 在寵物店

(C) 在旅行社 　　(D) 在百貨公司

▶說明 對話一開始男子打電話來詢問預訂機票的事，而女子則提供關於班機和票價的資訊，故可推知女子是在旅行社工作，故選 (C)。

B 66. Why is the man calling?

(A) To cancel his railway reservation

(B) To book a plane ticket

(C) To buy a small pet dog

(D) To inquire about the anniversary sale

男子為何打電話？

(A) 取消他的火車預訂

(B) 預訂機票

(C) 買小型寵物狗

(D) 詢問關於週年慶拍賣的事

▶說明 對話一開始男子就明確敘述他要預訂從波士頓飛往洛杉磯的機票，故選 (B)。

A 67. Look at the graphic. How much should the man pay additionally?

(A) $25 　　(B) $50

(C) $15 　　(D) $30

請看圖表。男子應該額外付多少費用？

(A) 二十五美元 　　(B) 五十美元

(C) 十五美元 　　(D) 三十美元

▶說明 對話後面男子提到他想帶小型寵物狗上飛機，而女子回應要另外付費，根據額外收費表所示，攜帶小型寵物要另外收二十五美元，故 (A) 是正確答案。

Questions 68–70 refer to the following conversation and itinerary.

W: We may need to talk about revising our itinerary for tomorrow's trip.

M: What do you think needs changing?

W: I'd like to spend more time at Bond Street. It's a famous shopping destination in the city.

M: Sure. Then how about staying there for two hours?

W: OK. I'm gonna buy some designer clothes. What would you want to buy there?

M: I have no idea now. Actually, I prefer window shopping.

請參考以下的對話及行程表回答**第 68 題至 70 題**。

女：我們可能需要討論一下修改明天行程的事。

男：你覺得哪裡需要修改呢？

女：我想在 Bond 街待久一些 。那是這個城市裡有名的一個購物景點。

男：好呀。那待兩個小時如何？

女：可以。我要買一些設計師品牌的服裝。你會想在那裡買什麼呢？

男：我現在不知道。其實我比較想逛逛櫥窗但不買東西。

時間	活動
7:30－8:00	早餐
8:10	前往 Ace 市
9:10－10:00	**312 博物館**
10:10－11:00	**Peace 教堂**
11:10－12:00	紀念公園
12:00－13:30	午餐
13:30－14:20	**Happy 歌劇院**
14:30－15:30	**Bond 街 (購物)**

15:30——回飯店

D **68.** Where does the woman want to stay longer?

(A) 312 Museum

(B) Monument Park

(C) Happy Opera House

(D) Bond Street

女子想在何處待久一些？

(A) 312 博物館　　(B) 紀念公園

(C) Happy 歌劇院　**(D) Bond 街**

▶說明 女子提到 "I'd like to spend more time at Bond Street."，故選 (D)。

B **69.** Look at the graphic. When will the speakers go back to the hotel?

(A) 3:30 p.m.　　**(B) 4:30 p.m.**

(C) 5:30 p.m.　　(D) 6:30 p.m.

請看圖表。說話者何時回飯店？

(A) 下午三點三十分

(B) 下午四點三十分

(C) 下午五點三十分

(D) 下午六點三十分

▶說明 對話中男子提到會在 Bond 街待兩個小時，而從圖表上可看出原本表訂時間是在 Bond 街從下午兩點半待到三點半，故修改後的行程應會在那裡待到四點半，也就是四點半回飯店，故選 (B)。

D **70.** What does the man prefer to buy?

(A) Clothes　　(B) Computers

(C) Windows　　**(D) Nothing**

男子較想要買什麼？

(A) 衣服　　　　(B) 電腦

(C) 窗戶　　　　**(D) 沒有**

▶說明 對話最後男子說他比較想要 "window shopping"，也就是逛街看看但不消費，故選 (D)。

PART 4

Questions 71–73 refer to the following telephone message.

This is Sandra Johnson from ABC Travel calling for Roger Campbell. I just looked at your travel request that you sent by e-mail. You said that you wanted 44 round-trip tickets from Taipei to Paris via Bangkok on May 4, returning on May 11. However, you only gave four names. Did you mean to reserve four tickets? Please call our office to confirm at your earliest convenience. We will be here in the office until 6 p.m. this evening, and your order number is NA3856. Thank you.

請參考以下的電話留言回答**第 71 題至 73 題**。
我是 ABC 旅遊的 Sandra Johnson，要找 Roger Campbell。我剛看了您透過電子郵件寄來的旅遊需求。您說您想要四十四張五月四日出發、五月十一日回來，從臺北經由曼谷轉機飛往巴黎的來回機票。然而您只提供了四個人的姓名。您是要預訂四張機票嗎？麻煩您盡快來電到我們辦公室確認。我們會在辦公室待到今晚六點，而您的訂票號碼是 NA3856。謝謝您。

B 71. Where does the speaker most likely work?

    (A) A hotel   **(B) A travel agency**
    (C) An airline   (D) A youth hostel

說話者最有可能在哪裡工作？

    (A) 飯店   **(B) 旅行社**
    (C) 航空公司   (D) 青年旅舍

▶說明 從電話留言第一至二句可知說話者在 ABC Travel 工作，剛收到顧客傳送的旅遊需求，故選 (B)。

A 72. Where will the customer travel to?

    (A) Paris   (B) Taipei
    (C) Bangkok   (D) Tokyo

顧客要到哪裡旅遊？

    (A) 巴黎   (B) 臺北
    (C) 曼谷   (D) 東京

▶說明 從留言第三句提到顧客想預訂從臺北經由曼谷轉機飛往巴黎的來回機票，

故答案為 (A)。

A 73. What does the speaker suggest the listener do?

    (A) Contact the office
    (B) Cancel the booking
    (C) Give 44 names
    (D) Change the itinerary

說話者建議聽者做什麼？

    (A) 聯絡辦公室
    (B) 取消預訂
    (C) 給四十四個姓名
    (D) 改變行程

▶說明 說話者提到 "Please call our office to confirm at your earliest convenience."，故答案為 (A)。

Questions 74–76 refer to the following announcement.

Welcome, and thank you everyone for attending this evening's art exhibition. We have prepared for the exhibition for one year. All of the artists are indigenous people. Their paintings and sculptures depict their lives and express their thoughts. We hope you will learn more about their culture through the artworks as you walk through these halls over the next few hours.

請參考以下的聲明回答**第 74 題至 76 題**。
歡迎以及感謝各位蒞臨今晚的藝術展覽。我們為了這個展覽籌劃了一年之久。所有參展的藝術家皆是原住民。他們的畫作和雕塑描繪了他們的生活並表達他們的思想。我們希望你們在接下來幾個小時在走廊參觀時，可以透過這些藝術作品更加瞭解他們的文化。

D 74. When is the announcement being made?

    (A) In the early morning
    (B) At lunchtime
    (C) In the afternoon
    (D) In the evening

聲明是何時發布的？

(A) 一大早 　　　(B) 午餐時間
(C) 下午 　　　**(D) 晚間**
▶說明 由於聲明一開始就說歡迎以及感謝各位蒞臨今晚的藝術展覽，故選 (D)。

C 75. How long did preparing for the exhibition take?

(A) One semester 　(B) Three months
(C) One year 　　(D) Three weeks

這次的展覽籌劃了多久時間？

(A) 一學期 　　　(B) 三個月
(C) 一年 　　　(D) 三個星期

▶說明 第二句提到這個展覽籌劃了一年之久，故選 (C)。

C 76. What does the speaker say about the artists?

(A) They are French.

(B) Their works are original.

(C) Their works express their thoughts.

(D) People can learn about their culture through the photos.

對於藝術家，說話者說了什麼？

(A) 他們是法國人。

(B) 他們的作品為原創的。

(C) 他們的作品表達他們的思想。

(D) 人們可以從這些相片更瞭解他們的文化。

▶說明 第四句提到他們的畫作和雕塑描繪了他們的生活並表達他們的思想，故選 (C)。

Questions 77–79 refer to the following speech.

We all know that CO2 is causing the world climate change and leads to global warming. Actually, everyone can do something to help reduce the emissions of CO2 into the atmosphere. For example, we can use energy-efficient light bulbs to save electricity at home. We can also use public transportation rather than drive to work.

Instead of riding a scooter to a convenience store in the neighborhood, why don't you just walk there? One person can't do a lot on his or her own, but if we all pitch in, we can help save the planet for our future generations.

請參考以下的演說回答**第 77 題至 79 題**。

我們都知道二氧化碳正造成世界氣候變遷並導致全球暖化。事實上，每個人都可以做點事來幫助減少二氧化碳排放至大氣中。舉例來說，我們在家可以使用省電燈泡來省電。我們也可利用大眾運輸工具而不是開車去上班。與其騎機車去附近的便利商店，你何不走路過去呢？一個人自己無法做很多事，但如果我們大家齊心協力，就可以為後代子孫幫忙拯救地球。

B 77. What is the speaker concerned about?

(A) Water pollution

(B) Global warming

(C) An energy crisis

(D) An economic issue

說話者在擔憂什麼？

(A) 水污染 　　　**(B) 全球暖化**
(C) 能源危機 　　(D) 經濟問題

▶說明 從演說第一句就提到二氧化碳正造成全世界氣候的變遷並導致全球暖化，故選 (B)。

C 78. What does the speaker advise listeners to do?

(A) Drive an electric car to work

(B) Pay attention to the current economic climate

(C) Use energy-efficient light bulbs

(D) Reduce the use of detergent

說話者建議聽者做什麼？

(A) 開電動車去上班

(B) 關注目前經濟情勢

(C) 使用省電燈泡

(D) 減少使用清潔劑

▶說明 從第三句說話者建議聽者可以使用省電燈泡，故選 (C)。

A 79. What does the speaker mean when

saying "if we all pitch in"?

(A) Everyone should do something for the earth.

(B) The government should adopt the right policy.

(C) Listeners should join the protest march.

(D) People should try to pitch the stone into the space.

當說話者說「如果我們大家齊心協力」，他想表達什麼意思？

(A) 每個人都應該為地球盡一份力。

(B) 政府應該採取正確的政策。

(C) 聽者應該加入抗議遊行。

(D) 人們應該試著將石頭扔到太空。

▶說明 "if we all pitch in" 的後面是 "we can help save the planet"，故選 (A)。

Questions 80–82 refer to the following telephone message.

Hello, Alan. This is Vivian Beckham from Human Resources. I'm calling because I have been assigned to arrange your upcoming business trip to Hong Kong, Thailand, and Indonesia. I need to arrange air tickets with the travel agent before I can make hotel and ground transportation reservations. So, I need your passport number and the exact name on your passport. Please call me back at your earliest convenience so that I can make the arrangements as soon as possible. Thank you.

請參考以下的電話留言回答**第 80 題至 82 題**。

Alan，你好。我是人力資源部的 Vivian Beckham。我打電話來是因為我被指派要安排你前往香港、泰國和印尼出差的相關事宜。在預訂旅館和地面交通之前，我需要先跟旅行社預訂機票。所以我需要你的護照號碼跟護照上的確切姓名。請盡速回電給我，這樣我才可以盡快安排。謝謝。

B 80. What is the message about?

(A) A long vacation

(B) A business trip

(C) An annual company trip

(D) A summer camp

此訊息是關於什麼？

(A) 長假　　　　**(B) 出差**

(C) 年度公司旅遊　(D) 夏令營

▶說明 從電話留言第三句就提到留言者打電話來是要安排 Alan 的出差相關事宜，故選 (B)。

C 81. Which of the following countries will Alan NOT go to?

(A) Thailand　　　(B) Hong Kong

(C) India　　　　(D) Indonesia

Alan 不會前往下列哪個國家？

(A) 泰國　　　　(B) 香港

(C) 印度　　　　(D) 印尼

▶說明 從電話留言第三句可知 Alan 即將要去香港、泰國和印尼出差，並未去印度，故選 (C)。

B 82. What does the speaker ask for?

(A) Ground transportation information

(B) Passport number and the name on the passport

(C) The names of the clients

(D) The phone number of the travel agent

說話者要求什麼東西？

(A) 地面交通資訊

(B) 護照號碼和護照上的名字

(C) 客戶的名字

(D) 旅行社的電話

▶說明 從留言第五句可知留言者向 Alan 索取他的護照號碼跟護照上的確切姓名，故選 (B)。

Questions 83–85 refer to the following news report.

This is Anna Lee reporting for Live Action 9 News. I am at the entrance to Modern

Electronics Store, where there is a long line of gamers waiting to purchase the latest version of Star Striker. The new game was released in many countries today. The long line stretches as far as we can see. It even goes around the corner to the next block! From the scene, it looks as if they were giving the games away. The 3–D graphics of the game are more realistic than ever, and every gaming magazine has given it top marks in their reviews. Looks like many parents may have more trouble than ever getting their kids to do their homework.

請參考以下的新聞報導回答**第 83 題至 85 題**。

以下是 Anna Lee 為實況行動九點新聞所做的報導。我現在正在 Modern 電子的入口處，這裡有大排長龍的電玩家等待購買最新版本的 Star Striker。這款新遊戲今天在許多國家發行。長長的隊伍延伸到我們目光所及。隊伍甚至到達下個街區的轉角處！這個景象看起來彷彿他們在免費贈送遊戲。這款遊戲的立體圖像比以往更具真實感，每一本電玩雜誌在評論中都給它極高的評價。看來許多父母要叫他們的孩子去做功課會比以往更加困難。

A 83. What is the speaker's job?

    (A) A television reporter

    (B) A video game salesperson

    (C) A game reviewer

    (D) A store manager

說話者的工作是什麼？

(A) 電視臺記者　　(B) 電玩業務

(C) 遊戲評論家　　(D) 店長

▶說明 從報導的一開頭說話者就提到 "This is Anna Lee reporting for Live Action 9 News."，可推知說話者是電視臺記者，故選 (A)。

D 84. Which of the following is NOT true?

    (A) The new game has been reviewed favorably.

    (B) The graphics of the new game are

better than its old version's.

    (C) There are a lot of people waiting in line to buy the game.

    (D) The new game is given away today.

下列何者有誤？

(A) 新遊戲獲得好評。

(B) 新遊戲的圖像比舊版本更棒。

(C) 有許多人排隊要購買遊戲。

(D) 新遊戲今天免費贈送。

▶說明 新聞報導提到 "it looks as if they were giving the games away"，這是與現在事實相反的假設語氣，故可知事實並非如此，故選 (D)。

D 85. What does the speaker say many parents may have difficulty doing?

    (A) Putting their children to bed

    (B) Entertaining their children

    (C) Stopping their children from using their cell phones

    (D) Asking their children to do their homework

說話者提到許多父母可能做什麼事情有困難？

(A) 哄孩子上床睡覺

(B) 娛樂孩子

(C) 阻止孩子使用手機

(D) 要求孩子去做功課

▶說明 新聞報導最後的結論是：有了這款新電玩，看來許多父母要叫他們的孩子去做功課會比以往更加困難，故選 (D)。

Questions 86–88 refer to the following talk.

We need to talk about this year's sales targets. Sales in North America and Europe have been stagnant for several years. It appears that we can't increase our sales any more in those regions. The Chinese market is largely untapped, but their government is making it difficult for us to market our products in the country. India is the fastest-growing market for us. To aggressively increase our market share there, we will be opening new branch offices in Kolkata and Chennai this year. We are also researching some countries in Africa such as South Africa, Nigeria, and Morocco. If we want to continue to boost our sales, it seems we will have to focus on India and Africa in the near future.

請參考以下的談話回答**第 86 題至 88 題**。

我們需要談論一下今年的銷售目標。北美和歐洲的銷售量已經停滯了好幾年。我們在那些地區似乎無法再增加銷量。中國市場有很多未開發的部分，但是他們的政府讓我們在其國家行銷產品產生困難。印度對我們來說是最快速成長的市場。我們今年會在加爾各答和清奈增設新的分部，以積極增加我們在那裡的市場佔有率。我們也會研究非洲一些國家，像是南非、奈及利亞和摩洛哥。如果我們想要持續提升我們的銷售量，未來似乎必須把重心放在印度跟非洲。

C 86. Which country seems to have no room for increasing sales?

(A) South Africa　　(B) Nigeria

(C) The USA　　(D) Morocco

以下哪一國家似乎沒有增加銷量的空間？

(A) 南非　　　　　(B) 奈及利亞

(C) 美國　　　　(D) 摩洛哥

▶**說明** 根據談話第二至三句提到，北美的銷售量已經停滯了好幾年且似乎無法再增加銷量，故選 (C)。

D 87. What is the problem with the Chinese market?

(A) There are no branch offices in China.

(B) Sales in China have been stagnant for several years.

(C) People there are not interested in luxury goods.

(D) Its government makes it hard to promote the products there.

中國市場有什麼問題？

(A) 在中國沒有分部。

(B) 在中國的銷售量已經停滯好幾年。

(C) 那裡的人們對奢侈品不感興趣。

(D) 它的政府使在那裡推廣產品不易。

▶**說明** 談話第四句指出，中國市場雖然有很多未開發的部分，但其政府讓他們在中國行銷產品增加困難度，故選 (D)。

A 88. In which area is the company going to open new branch offices this year?

(A) India　　　　(B) America

(C) Europe　　　　(D) Africa

這間公司今年將在哪個地區新增分部？

(A) 印度　　　　(B) 美洲

(C) 歐洲　　　　　(D) 非洲

▶**說明** 談話第五句及第六句提到公司今年將會在印度的加爾各答和清奈增設新的分部，故選 (A)。

Questions 89–91 refer to the following telephone message.

Hi, Takashi. This is Maggie Barry calling. Thank you so much for helping at the office party last night. Everyone is still raving about the Japanese dishes that you prepared for the party. The sushi rolls were very delicious. In addition, the sashimi was tasty with the wasabi not too spicy. I think the Japanese dishes were the most popular ones. Anyway, see you on Monday. And if you want to bring some sushi rolls with you, I wouldn't mind. Ha!

請參考以下的電話留言回答**第 89 題至 91 題**。

嗨，Takashi，我是 Maggie Barry。非常感謝你幫忙昨晚的辦公室派對。每個人仍在對你為派對準備的日式料理讚不絕口。壽司捲非常美味。此外，生魚片搭配不太辣的芥末非常好吃。我認為日式料理是最受青睞的。總之，星期一見。你如果想帶一些壽司捲來，我是不會介意的。哈哈！

B 89. What is the purpose of the message?

(A) To make a request

(B) To express gratitude

(C) To offer congratulations

(D) To give some advice

留言的目的為何？

(A) 提出請求　　　**(B) 表達感謝**

(C) 表示恭喜　　　(D) 給予建議

▶說明 留言第三句提到非常感謝對方幫忙辦公室派對，故選 (B)。

C 90. What did Takashi help prepare at the party?

(A) The music　　　(B) The invitations

(C) The dishes　　(D) The decorations

Takashi 在派對上幫忙準備什麼？

(A) 音樂　　　　　(B) 邀請卡

(C) 料理　　　　(D) 裝飾

▶說明 電話留言第四句提到每個人對 Takashi 為派對準備的日式料理讚不絕口，故選 (C)。

D 91. What does the speaker hope that Takashi will do on Monday?

(A) Prepare for another party

(B) Have dinner with her

(C) Start to teach her Japanese

(D) Bring some sushi rolls

說話者希望 Takashi 在星期一做什麼？

(A) 準備另一場派對

(B) 跟她一起吃晚餐

(C) 開始教她日文

(D) 帶一些壽司捲

▶說明 說話者最後說如果 Takashi 星期一想帶一些壽司捲來，她是很歡迎的，故選 (D)。

Questions 92–94 refer to the following announcement.

Good morning. Welcome to Pine State National Park. I'm Victor Smith and will be your guide today. There are a total of four trails in the park. It's a pity that two of them are marked "off limits" because of recent landslides. So, I will take you to the other two trails. Be careful when you walk along them as some snakes were spotted there last month. You might be startled if you see them, but there is nothing to be afraid of since they are not dangerous. This hike will take about three hours in total. By the way, here is some bug repellent. You will definitely need it with many mosquitoes and insects out today.

請參考以下的聲明回答**第 92 題至 94 題**。

早安。歡迎蒞臨 Pine State 國家公園。我是你們今天的導覽員 Victor Smith。這座公園裡總共有四條步道。可惜的是，其中兩條因為最近土石流的緣故被標示「禁止進入」。所以我將帶領你們去另外兩條步道。當你們走這兩條步道時要小心，因為上個月有一些蛇被發現在那裡出沒。你們看到牠們時可能會嚇一跳，但是沒什麼好怕的，因為牠們不具危險性。這趟健行總共會需要大約三個小時。對了，這裡有一些驅蟲劑。今天有這麼多蚊子和昆蟲出沒，你們絕對會需要驅蟲劑。

B 92. Who is the announcement for?

(A) Park rangers　　**(B) Tourists**

(C) Bus drivers　　(D) Security guards

此聲明的主要對象是誰？

(A) 公園管理者　　**(B) 觀光客**

(C) 公車司機　　　(D) 警衛

▶說明 從聲明前三句的歡迎詞和導覽員的自我介紹，可推知他在和一群觀光客談話，故選 (B)。

C 93. Why are two of the trails marked "off limits"?

(A) There are dangerous snakes there.

(B) They are too difficult for novice hikers.

(C) Landslides happened there recently.

(D) There are infected mosquitoes there.

為何其中兩條步道被標示「禁止進入」？
(A) 那裡有危險的蛇類。
(B) 這些步道對新手健行者太困難。
(C) 那裡最近發生土石流。
(D) 那裡有病媒蚊。

▶說明 聲明第五句提到其中兩條步道因為最近土石流的緣故被標示「禁止進入」，故選 (C)。

A 94. What does the speaker give to the listeners?

(A) Bug repellent (B) Maps

(C) Pesticide (D) Bottled water

說話者給聽者什麼東西？

(A) 驅蟲劑 (B) 地圖

(C) 殺蟲劑 (D) 瓶裝水

▶說明 從聲明最後兩句可知導覽員提供觀光客一些驅蟲劑以防止被蚊蟲叮咬，故選 (A)。

Questions 95–97 refer to the following advertisement and agenda.

Do you want to improve your performance at work? Do you want to increase your productivity? Why not sign up for our workshop "Be Super Productive at Work"? We've invited highly qualified speakers who will inspire you and give you practical advice through three speeches. We will also offer consultant meetings during the breakout session, when you can discuss your situations with experts. You would regret it if you miss this chance. Access our website to check out the workshop agenda at www.careersuccess.com.

請參考以下的廣告及時程表回答**第 95 題至 97 題**。

想改善你的工作表現嗎？想增加你的生產力嗎？何不報名我們的「職場超級高效能」工作坊？我們已邀請深具資格的講者，他們將透過三場演說啟發你並給你實用的建議。我們也會在分組時段提供顧問會談，讓你可以和專家討論自己的狀況。錯過這次機會，你會後悔的。查詢工作坊時程表，請到我們的網站 www.careersuccess.com。

職場超級高效能	
10:00–10:30	歡迎及介紹
10:30–12:00	必要的時間管理技巧
12:00–13:00	午餐
13:00–14:30	專注
14:30–15:30	分組時間
15:30–17:00	盡可能快樂

C 95. What does the speaker say about the workshop?

(A) It offers refreshments during the breakout session.

(B) People should sign up as soon as possible.

(C) The speakers will give useful advice.

(D) Attendees need to fill out a comment card online.

關於工作坊，說話者說了什麼？

(A) 工作坊在分組時間提供點心。

(B) 人們應該盡快報名。

(C) 講者將給予有用的建議。

(D) 參加者需要線上填寫意見單。

▶說明 說話者提到講者會給予 "practical advice"，也就是有用的建議，故選 (C)。

D 96. Look at the graphic. When are the consultant meetings offered?

(A) 10:30–12:00 (B) 12:00–13:00

(C) 13:00–14:30 **(D) 14:30–15:30**

請看圖表。顧問會談在何時提供？

(A) 10:30–12:00 (B) 12:00–13:00

(C) 13:00–14:30 **(D) 14:30–15:30**

▶說明 說話者提到會在分組時段提供顧問會談，而圖表上顯示分組時段為 14:30–15:30，故選 (D)。

C 97. Where can listeners find the agenda?

(A) A brochure (B) A poster

(C) A website (D) A bulletin board

聽者可以在何處找到時程表？
(A) 小冊子 　　　　(B) 海報
(C) 網站 　　　　(D) 佈告欄
▶說明 說話者最後提到要查詢工作坊時程表請到他們的網站，故選 (C)。

Questions 98–100 refer to the following telephone message.

Hello, Alison, this is Joseph Madison calling. The HR manager has told me that the Product Development Department will have five new employees next month, including one new manager, so we should make sure that there's enough furniture for their new office on the third floor of the King Building. Please check that the new office has at least ten desks and chairs along with the necessary office equipment. The new manager will come next Friday. I hope you can have everything ready by then.

請參考以下的電話留言回答**第 98 題至 100 題**。

你好，Alison，我是 Joseph Madison。人事經理告訴我產品發展部門下個月將會有五位新員工，包括一位新的經理，所以我們需要確定他們在國王大樓三樓的新辦公室有足夠的傢俱。麻煩檢查一下，新的辦公室至少要有十套桌椅以及必要的辦公室用品。新的經理下週五會來。我希望你在那之前可以把一切準備妥當。

新辦公室設備清單
■ 桌子：八張
■ 椅子：十二張
■ 電話：兩臺
■ 傳真機：一臺
■ 電腦：八臺
■ 印表機：兩臺

D 98. Who is most likely the speaker?
(A) Product manager
(B) Accounting manager
(C) Warehouse manager
(D) General affairs manager

說話者最有可能是誰？
(A) 產品經理 　　　　(B) 會計經理
(C) 倉儲經理 　　　　**(D) 總務經理**
▶說明 根據電話留言內容，說話者主要在指示 Alison 去確認新的辦公室的設備是否齊全，可推知說話者可能屬於總務部門，故選 (D)。

C 99. How many workers are expected to use the new office?
(A) 5 　　　　(B) 6
(C) 10 　　　　(D) 11
新的辦公室預計有多少職員使用？
(A) 五位 　　　　(B) 六位
(C) 十位 　　　　(D) 十一位
▶說明 留言第三句提到需要至少十套桌椅，故可推知新的辦公室將有十位職員使用，故選 (C)。

C 100. Look at the graphic. What will Alison have to order for the new office?
(A) One chair 　　(B) One fax machine
(C) Two desks 　(D) Two printers
請看圖表。Alison 必須為新辦公室訂購什麼？
(A) 一張椅子 　　　(B) 一臺傳真機
(C) 兩張桌子 　　(D) 兩臺印表機
▶說明 留言第三句提到需要有十套桌椅，而根據清單內容，桌子只有八張，故需要再訂兩張桌子才夠用，故選 (C)。

PART 5

C 101. Sally 在她的主管到達前十分鐘就應該到達。

(A) 她自己 (反身代名詞)　　　　　　　　(B) 她 (主格代名詞)

(C) 她的 (所有格形容詞)　　　　　　　(D) 她的 (所有格代名詞)

▶說明 空格後面是名詞 supervisor，因此可推知空格內要選擇所有格 her 來修飾這個名詞，故答案為 (C)。

A 102. 法國的美食舉世聞名。

(A) 食物的　　　　(B) 有利的　　　　(C) 拖延的　　　　(D) 古怪的

▶說明 culinary delights 是美食的意思，其他選項的字彙若填入空格皆語意不通，故正確答案為 (A)。

B 103. Anderson 先生的公司既販賣低價品也販賣奢侈品。

(A) 每個　　　**(B) 兩者都**　　　(C) 任一個　　　(D) 不僅

▶說明 在句子後半段用對等連接詞 and 連接了 low-priced goods 和 luxury goods 這兩個名詞片語，而 "both A and B" 的句型意即「A 和 B 兩者都有」，故 (B) 為合理的答案。

D 104. Neil Adams 被董事長任命為首席執行長。

(A) 任命 (過去式)　　　　　　　　(B) 任命 (不定詞)

(C) 任命 (過去進行式)　　　　　　**(D) 被任命 (過去被動式)**

▶說明 由於在空格後面為 by the chairman，可判斷空格前是被動語態，意為「被任命」，故正確答案為 (D)。nominate 有提名和任命兩個字義，此處應為任命。

B 105. NBA 決賽的現場直播將很快開始。

(A) 從來　　　**(B) 很快**　　　(C) 還沒　　　(D) 因此

▶說明 由句意來判斷，本句是指 NBA 決賽的現場實況轉播就要開始了，故 (B) 為合理的選項。

C 106. 這位導遊建議遊客，在此地不要夜間獨自外出。

(A) 去 (過去式)　　(B) 去 (不定詞)　　**(C) 去 (原形動詞)**　　(D) 去 (現在分詞)

▶說明 本題所考的是 advise 的用法，當 advise 後面接 that 引導的名詞子句當受詞時，其句型為 "S1 advise that S2 (should) VR. . . ."，因此後面名詞子句內要使用原形動詞，故正確答案為 (C)。

A 107. 暴風雨比預期還早來到，我們淋得濕透了。

(A) 較早 (副詞比較級) (B) 早 (副詞原級)　　(C) 早 (名詞)　　(D) 最早 (副詞最高級)

▶說明 由於在空格後面有連接詞 than，因此可推知前面必須使用比較級，故正確答案為 (A)。

B 108. 由於暴風雪突然來襲，店家今天在早上十一點半開始營業而不是十點。

(A) 儘管　　　**(B) 而不是**　　　(C) 無論　　　(D) 因為

▶說明 句子前半段提到暴風雪突然來襲，因此可推知可能的文意是店家今天十一點半開始營業，「而不是」平常的十點，故 (B) 為合理的答案。

D 109. 飛機因機場的強風而延後起飛。

(A) 出發 (原形動詞)　(B) 出發 (過去式)　(C) 出發 (現在分詞)　**(D) 出發 (名詞)**

▶說明 因為空格前面有定冠詞 the，而且空格後面有介系詞片語 of the plane，因此可以判斷空格應填入名詞，故正確答案為 (D)。

A 110. Josh 寧可自己做這個任務也不想和他的同事合作。

(A) 合作 (原形動詞)　(B) 合作 (過去分詞)　(C) 合作 (名詞)　(D) 合作的 (形容詞)

▶說明 本題所考的是 "would rather VR1 than VR2" 的句型，表示「寧願做 V1，也不要做 V2」，因此空格處要填入原形動詞，故正確答案為 (A)。

C 111. 我們確信我們的團隊有很大的機會能夠簽下這份合約。

(A) 少見地　(B) 一點都不　**(C) 非常**　(D) 遠地

▶說明 依句意判斷可以得知應該是一個「非常」好的機會，故正確答案為 (C)。

B 112. 如果你已付過入場費，那麼你就不用付其他的費用。

(A) 雖然　**(B) 那麼**　(C) 甚至　(D) 但是

▶說明 then 為副詞，"If . . . then. . . ." 句型的意思是「如果…那麼…」，因此 (B) 是合理的答案。

B 113. 你確定那座小教堂可以容納兩百名賓客嗎？

(A) 附著　**(B) 容納**　(C) 加速　(D) 使熟悉

▶說明 在 that 子句中的主詞是 the small church，是一個「場所」；空格後面是 two hundred guests，是「人」，因此可以聯想是指某個場所能夠「容納」的人數，故正確答案為 (B)。

C 114. 現今，人們的日常生活中不能沒有電燈。

(A) 電子的　(B) 電力　**(C) 使用電的**　(D) 電子學

▶說明 因為空格後面是名詞 lights，故空格應填入形容詞，加上由句意可以推斷應該是指「電」燈，故正確答案為 (C)。

D 115. 我們需要修改計畫，因為客戶直到明天才會抵達。

(A) 儘管　(B) 除非　(C) 在…上　**(D) 直到…才…**

▶說明 由句型結構與句意來判斷，本句是在考 "not . . . until. . . ." 的句型，意即「直到…才…」，故正確答案為 (D)。

B 116. Joshua Roberts 接替 Bella Watson 擔任公司總裁。

(A) 權威　**(B) 繼任者**　(C) 祖先　(D) 後代

▶說明 句中提到擔任公司總裁，故只有 (B) 是合理的答案。"be the successor to sb as" 意為「接替某人擔任某職務」。

C 117. 公司正試圖把業務擴展到東南亞。

(A) 沿著　(B) 之間　**(C) 進入**　(D) 隨著

▶說明 句中使用了動詞 expand，意指「擴張」、「發展」，要搭配 into 這個介系詞來表示「擴展到…領域或地區當中」，故正確答案為 (C)。

A 118. 實驗室的研究人員已開發出一種能發現人體內缺陷基因的方法。

(A) 方法　(B) 症狀　(C) 療法　(D) 分配

▶說明 此句使用的動詞是 develop，意指「發展、開發」，而在空格後面的句意為發現人體內的缺陷基因，因此可推知前面的意思是開發出一種新的「方法」，故 (A) 為合理的答案。

B 119. Justin Reeves 自己是一位成功的演員，所以他深知要演得好是多麼不容易。

(A) 他 (主格代名詞)　　　　　　　　　**(B) 他自己 (反身代名詞)**

(C) 他 (受格)　　　　　　　　　　　　(D) 他的 (所有格形容詞)

▶說明 由於句子結構已經完整，再加上依句意來判斷，推知空格處可用反身代名詞 himself 來加強語氣，表示「他自己本身」，故正確答案為 (B)。

D 120. 經理很賞識我們對於發展這項新產品所做的貢獻。

(A) 捐贈者　　　　　　　　　　　　　(B) 促成的

(C) 貢獻 (第三人稱單數動詞)　　　　　**(D) 貢獻 (名詞)**

▶說明 由於空格前面是定冠詞 the，空格後面由句型判斷可知是一個關係子句，因此可以判斷空格內應填入名詞，而 make contributions 意為「作出貢獻」，故正確答案為 (D)。

D 121. 管理階層鼓勵業務部門超越去年的業績表現。

(A) 討價還價　　　　(B) 最小化　　　　(C) 通知　　　　　**(D) 超越**

▶說明 題目中提到了 "encouraged . . . to. . . ."，表示「鼓勵某人去做…」，而空格後提到去年的業績表現，因此可推知是鼓勵去「超越」去年的業績表現，故 (D) 為合理的答案。

B 122. 城市的市民正期盼新地鐵線的完工。

(A) 完成 (原形動詞)　**(B) 完成 (名詞)**　(C) 完全地 (副詞)　(D) 完成 (過去分詞)

▶說明 題目中空格前面是定冠詞 the，後面是介系詞片語 of the new metro line，因此可判斷空格應填入名詞，故正確答案為 (B)。

A 123. 粉絲們在排隊等候拿偶像的親筆簽名時感到很興奮。

(A) 當…時　　　　　(B) 或者　　　　　(C) 除了　　　　　(D) 可是

▶說明 空格前提到粉絲們很興奮，空格後提到他們排隊等候拿偶像的親筆簽名，因此推知空格可填入「當…時」，故 (A) 為合理的答案。

C 124. 想知道計畫細節的人可以在開會時詢問 Sarah Smith 或在這週任何時候寄電子郵件給她。

(A) 她 (主格代名詞)　　　　　　　　　(B) 他們的 (所有格形容詞)

(C) 她 (受格代名詞)　　　　　　　　(D) 他們 (主格代名詞)

▶說明 由於在句子前半段提到了 Sarah Smith 女士，因此後面的文意是指可以在任何時間寄電子郵件給「她」，故正確答案為 (C)。

C 125. 雖然多數人認為 Rivera 先生對於這份工作太缺乏經驗，但結果證明他是這份工作的絕佳人選。

(A) 額外的　　　　　(B) 很可能的　　　**(C) 缺乏經驗的**　　(D) 可信的

▶說明 句子以 Even though 開始，表示「雖然、即使」，而後面提到 turned out，表示出現了一種出乎意料的情況，也就是 Rivera 先生是這份工作的絕佳人選一事是出乎意料的，因此可推知原本多數人並不看好他，故 (C) 為合理的答案。

D 126. 我們將需要審查你與客戶之間往來的所有電子郵件以確定你有充分的溝通能力。

(A) 相稱　　　　　　(B) 記者　　　　　(C) 相應的　　　　**(D) 通信**

▶說明 因為空格前提到了 email，空格後提到 with the clients，因此可推知是和客戶之間的電子郵件「通信」，故正確答案為 (D)。

B 127. 微波爐和冰箱是現代廚房很常見的家用電器。

(A) 條件 　　　　　(B) 器具 　　　　　(C) 航站 　　　　　(D) 遺跡

▶說明 句子前半段提到微波爐和冰箱，這兩項都是很常見的家電，故正確答案為 (B)。家電是 household appliances 或 domestic appliances。

A 128. 一旦你報名了這門課程，就無法再取消註冊。

(A) 一旦 　　　　　(B) 總是 　　　　　(C) 關於 　　　　　(D) 是否

▶說明 句子前半段提到報名了這個課程，後面提到無法取消註冊，因此可推知是指「一旦」報名課程就不能取消，故正確答案為 (A)。

C 129. 道路上的積雪已造成駕駛和行人的許多不便。

(A) 制裁 　　　　　(B) 持續時間 　　　　　**(C) 堆積** 　　　　　(D) 程序

▶說明 空格後面提到 on the roads，而且也提到對駕駛和行人造成許多問題，因此 (C) 是合理的答案，snow accumulation 意為「積雪」。

B 130. 如果你無法準時抵達，請事先來電告知我們。

(A) 在⋯之後 　　　　　**(B) 如果** 　　　　　(C) 除了 　　　　　(D) 在此期間

▶說明 句子前半段提到無法準時抵達，後面提到請事先打電話，可以判斷前面是一種「條件」或「情況」，因此要用 if 來表達，故 (B) 為合理的答案。

PART 6

請參考以下的信件回答**第 131 題至 134 題**。

親愛的 Jones 先生：

謝謝您訂購我們的空氣品質偵測器。現在愈來愈多人關心所呼吸的空氣的品質並想予以控制。遺憾的是，雖然您訂購的偵測器機型仍有庫存，但您指定的灰色樣式目前沒有庫存。大概一個月後我們才會收到另一批貨。如果您願意，您可以選擇不同的顏色便能立即配送。其他的選擇有黑色、白色、藍色和紅色。或者您也可以等一個月。請盡早回覆此信告知您的決定。

致上誠摯的問候，

Jessica Flint
CGI 科技客戶服務部

B 131. (A) 的 　　　　　**(B) 對於** 　　　　　(C) 在 　　　　　(D) 與

▶說明 "be concerned about sth." 意指「關心某事」，故正確答案為 (B)。

C 132. (A) 我們以後不會再製造灰色的樣式。

(B) 我們沒有計畫之後再次銷售它們。

(C) 大概一個月後我們才會收到另一批貨。

(D) 你可以從我們的型錄中挑選任一種型號。

▶說明 空格前面的句子提到，雖然 Mr. Jones 所訂的機型有存貨，但是他所要求的顏色卻是缺貨狀態，可推知應填入空格的句子會針對此狀況有所說明，而 (C) 提到可能要過一個月左右才會再進貨，正好符合此處的文意脈絡，故為正確答案。

D 133. (A) 合適的 　　　　　(B) 出色的 　　　　　(C) 鮮明的 　　　　　**(D) 不同的**

▶說明 Mr. Jones 本來訂的灰色已經缺貨，而本題後面再次提到 color 這個字，可見是指「不同的」顏色，故正確答案為 (D)。

A 134. (A) 回覆   (B) 要求   (C) 等待   (D) 刪除

▶說明 因為空格後面為介系詞 to，而且受詞為 this letter，因此可推知是指「回覆」此封信件，故正確答案為 (A)。

請參考以下的公告回答**第 135 題至 138 題**。

> 綠線兩個車站的施工在未來兩週將對鐵路交通造成影響。South Street 站及 Smith Street 站將會在這兩週關閉。雖然列車會繼續行駛，但有時可能會因施工而延誤。如果您可搭另一線到達您的目的地，強烈建議您考慮改搭替代路線。我們為此不便致歉。希望施工所帶來更好的服務能對此有所彌補。

C 135. (A) 造成 (過去分詞)   (B) 造成 (第三人稱單數動詞)

      (C) 將造成 (未來式)   (D) 造成 (過去進行式)

▶說明 此句最後提到 "for the next two weeks"，表示這是指未來的一段時間，因此動詞要使用未來式，故正確答案為 (C)。

A 136. (A) 雖然   (B) 除了   (C) 每當   (D) 儘管

▶說明 此句前半段提到列車將會繼續行駛，後半段則提到可能因為工程而延誤，因此可推知前後子句之間在文意上有「對比」或「反差」，必須用 while 這個連接詞來表達此種轉折，故正確答案為 (A)。

B 137. (A) 目標   **(B) 目的地**   (C) 目的   (D) 成果

▶說明 文章內容與搭乘火車有關，而此句提到搭乘替代路線，因此可以推知是去「目的地」，故正確答案為 (B)。

C 138. (A) 他們會努力工作以得到獎金。   (B) 工程將比預定提早完成。

      (C) 我們為此不便致歉。   (D) 這在接下來兩週會發生。

▶說明 空格後的句子提到更好的服務能對此有所彌補，因此可推知填入空格的句子應表達了歉意，故 (C) 為合理的答案。

請參考以下的文章回答**第 139 題至 142 題**。

> 各位跑者，歡迎來到這座城市。身為本市的市長，看見你們來參加我們的馬拉松，我感到很高興且榮幸。這是一項令我們驕傲的賽事。當你們在這個城市跑著這四十二點二公里的路程，全體市民都會祝福你們。
>
> 你們在本市停留時，也可以趁此機會造訪我們的城市的景點。我們有舉世聞名的動物園及美麗的水岸，水岸邊有商店街及許多供應各種當地特色菜的餐館。此外，我們的美術館也值得一去。它收藏大量的現代藝術作品。
>
> 非常謝謝你們來。我希望你們在此過得愉快並祝你們在馬拉松賽拿到好成績。

C 139. (A) 你們需要繳交報名費用。   (B) 我鼓勵你們在本市多待一會。

      (C) 這是一項令我們驕傲的賽事。   (D) 讓我來解釋為什麼我們要辦這場比賽。

▶說明 空格前表示對馬拉松跑者的歡迎，空格後表示對馬拉松跑者的祝福之意，因此可推知空格應填入的句子與馬拉松賽事必定相關，而四個選項中僅有 (C) 放入此脈絡能連貫前後文意，故正確答案為 (C)。

B 140. (A) 觀點　　　　　　　**(B) 機會**　　　　　(C) 資格　　　　　(D) 責任

▶說明 此句提到跑者可以去參觀城市的景點，可以推知是把握「機會」去做這件事，故合理的答案為 (B)。

A 141. **(A) 供應 (現在分詞)**　(B) 供應 (過去分詞)　(C) 供應 (原形動詞)　(D) 伺服器

▶說明 此句可寫成 ". . . many restaurants which serve various local specialties." 把其中的關係子句省略後，留下 serving 這個主動式分詞片語來修飾原本的先行詞 restaurants，故正確答案為 (A)。

B 142. (A) 確切的說　　　　　**(B) 此外**　　　　　(C) 儘管如此　　　　(D) 直到那時

▶說明 空格前介紹了動物園等城市裡的景點，空格後開始介紹另一個景點，故正確答案為 (B)，additionally 在此具有承上啟下的轉承作用。

請參考以下的信件回答**第 143 題至 146 題**。

Roger Foster

Robinson 工程公司

Ford 大道二十一號

蒙特婁，魁北克

親愛的 Foster 先生：

我代表比賽委員會的全體同仁恭喜您獲得參加加拿大工業設計比賽的資格。只有全加拿大最優秀的設計師們能獲得參加此比賽的資格。您的成就是您和貴公司的重大榮譽。

要贏過其他優秀的設計師是極具挑戰性的。我們祝您好運。您在十一月二十二日將需要在艾德蒙頓進行報告，展示您的設計模型。隨函附上您之後預訂機票及在艾德蒙頓的住宿所需要的資訊。若您需要任何協助，請立刻寄電子郵件給我。

祝好，

Joseph Basil

比賽委員會委員

加拿大工業設計比賽

C 143. (A) 恭喜 (原形動詞)　　　　　　　(B) 恭喜 (第三人稱單數動詞)

(C) 恭喜 (不定詞)　　　　　　　　(D) 恭喜 (名詞)

▶說明 此題所測驗的用法是 "would like to VR"，意指「想要」、「打算」，故正確答案為 (C)。

D 144. (A) 優先考慮的事　　(B) 移動　　　　(C) 代表　　　　**(D) 成就**

▶說明 從此句文意可推知空格應填入的詞彙是可以作為重大榮譽的事物，而從前文可知此事物應是獲得比賽資格的這一項「成就」，故正確答案為 (D)。

A 145. (A) 我們祝您好運。　　　　　　　　　　(B) 我花費了許多功夫。

(C) 他們必須面對這個挑戰。　　　　　　(D) 請安排地上交通事宜。

▶說明 空格前 Joseph Basil 告訴 Foster 先生這項比賽的困難度，故根據此脈絡僅有 (A) 為合理的答案。

B 146. (A) 儘管　　　　　　**(B) 以及**　　　　　　(C) 因為　　　　　　(D) 相較於

▶說明 空格前提到 Foster 先生需要預訂機票，而空格前後是對等的兩個名詞，因此可推知是預定機票「以及」預定住宿，故正確答案為 (B)。

PART 7

請參考以下的廣告回答**第 147 題至 148 題**。

徵兼職廚師

Darren's 牛排館正在尋找兼職廚師。不需要經驗。我們在找的人只需要敬業、具學習心並飽有能在繁忙的廚房工作的幹勁。平日兩到三個晚上及假日必須能來上班。這個工作很適合學生。我們的班表具彈性。 最重要的是 ， 我們提供員工優渥的薪資及大筆獎金。 意者請親自前來 Main Street 店找廚房經理應徵。

A 147. 應徵此工作需要多少工作經驗？

(A) 無　　　　　　(B) 六個月　　　　　　(C) 一年　　　　　　(D) 兩年

▶說明 在廣告中第二句提到 "No experience is needed." 可知這個工作不要求工作經驗，故正確答案為 (A)。

D 148. 關於此工作，下列何者不正確？

(A) 廚師可能需要在週末上班。　　　　　(B) 工作環境的事情繁多。

(C) 待遇不錯。　　　　　　　　　　　　**(D) 班表是固定的。**

▶說明 在廣告中倒數第三句提到 "We have flexible schedules"，可知這份工作的時間表是彈性的、不是固定的，因此正確答案為 (D)。

請參考以下的簡訊對話紀錄回答**第 149 題至 150 題**。

Sally Moore	十五點二十二分

你這週六會去國際會議嗎？

| Andrew Martin | 十五點二十二分 |

是的。

| Sally Moore | 十五點二十三分 |

你會議結束後有空嗎？我想談談新的專案。

| Andrew Martin | 十五點二十四分 |

沒問題。會議中午結束，而我的班機是三點半。我們可以一起去吃午飯然後討論。

| Sally Moore | 十五點二十五分 |

好主意。我可以在那裡的一家餐廳預訂午餐的位子。

| Andrew Martin | 十五點二十五分 |

感謝！

| Sally Moore | 十五點二十六分 |

週六見。

C 149. 關於 Martin 先生，文中提到了什麼？

(A) 他不會參加會議。 　　　　　　　　　(B) 他的班機晚上起飛。

(C) 他將和 Moore 女士討論專案。 　　(D) 他將預訂午餐的位子。

▶說明 第三則簡訊中 Moore 女士表示想討論新的專案 ， 第四則簡訊中 Msrtin 先生答應了 Moore 女士，故正確答案為 (C)。

B 150. 會議是何時？

(A) 這週六下午 　　**(B) 這週六早上** 　　(C) 這週六傍晚 　　(D) 這週六晚上

▶說明 第一則簡訊提到會議是在這週六舉行，第四則簡訊提到會議到中午結束，可推知會議時間是在這週六早上，故正確答案為 (B)。

請參考以下的訂購單回答**第 151 題至 152 題**。

Barbara's 衣服修改店

訂單編號：BE–354

收件日期：七月九日

客戶：Albert Davis

連絡電話：0911123456

物件：黃色運動衫一件

修改：在運動衫上繡上「Albert Davis」及「第一百場馬拉松」的字樣

文字顏色：藍

取件日期：七月二十五日

修改人：Susan Swade

C 151. Albert Davis 想修改什麼？

(A) 他潛水時穿的服裝 　　　　　　　(B) 他滑雪時穿的夾克

(C) 他跑步時穿的上衣 　　　　　　(D) 他健行時穿的毛衣

▶說明 訂購單上的 alteration 欄位內容提到要在運動衫繡上「第一百場馬拉松」的字樣，可推知是跑馬拉松時穿的運動衫，故正確答案為 (C)。

B 152. Susan Swade 最有可能是什麼身份？

(A) 跑者 　　　　　**(B) 裁縫** 　　　　(C) 駕駛 　　　　(D) 畫家

▶說明 訂購單最後一欄提到衣服被指定由 Susan Swade 修改，可推知她最有可能是這家店的一名裁縫，故正確答案為 (B)。

請參考以下的電子郵件回答**第 153 題至 154 題**。

寄件人：Amanda Black <ablack@activeclothing.com>

收件人：Frank Sampson <fsampson@appleton.com>

回覆：T 恤

日期：九月十七日

親愛的 Sampson 先生：

謝謝您詢問關於購買我們公司 T 恤的問題。我們對於 T 恤的品質以及您想放在隊服上的圖樣設計品質作出保證。請看下列的價目表，並讓我知道您的隊伍想要什麼。請在您的訂單內具體指出需要的袖型、設計、顏色以及尺寸。

袖型	顏色		
長袖 T 恤：每件十二元	紅、黃、藍、白、黑、綠		
短袖 T 恤：每件八元	其他：_____		
	尺寸		
設計	特小：_____件		小：_____件
公司內部設計：每小時工資七十元*	中：_____件		大：_____件
印製 T 恤：每件二元	特大：_____件		

*非必要。客戶可自己提供設計。

附註：1. 訂單超過五十件的客戶享有九折優惠。

　　　2. 運費另計。

　　　3. 若符合課稅條件將會被當地課稅。

若您有任何疑問，請不吝詢問。

致上誠摯的問候，

Amanda Black

團購部門

Active 服裝股份有限公司

B 153. Black 女士為什麼要寫這封 e-mail？

　　(A) 為了投訴一項產品　　　　　　　　　**(B) 為了寄送資訊給潛在買家**

　　(C) 為了訂購一件 T 恤　　　　　　　　　(D) 為了招募新員工

　　▶說明 信中第一句表示感謝對方來信詢問購買 T 恤，可知對方是潛在買家，信件後面提出價格清單，可知這封信的目的是讓潛在買家瞭解價格等資訊，故正確答案為 (B)。

D 154. 客戶被允許可提供什麼？

　　(A) 襯衫　　　　　　(B) 設備　　　　　　(C) 優惠　　　　　　**(D) 設計**

　　▶說明 價目表的 Design 欄位提到："Customers can provide the design on their own."，可知顧客也可以自己提供 T-shirt 上面的圖樣設計，故正確答案為 (D)。

請參考以下的文章回答**第 155 題至 157 題**。

洛杉磯 (七月十五日)──Cookie Fantastic 月底將在加州市場上推出新口味的餅乾。 奶茶口味的夾心內餡將是此新系列餅乾的主要特色。

公司總裁 Adrian Meldane 注意到本州龐大的華裔美籍人口，並發現許多華裔美國人喜歡奶茶口味的產品。他也注意到奶茶不只在亞洲人的社區受歡迎，在大洛杉磯地區也同樣受歡迎。[1] 讓總裁相信新產品可能會成功的另一原因，則是由於另一家本地公司所出品的奶茶口味冰淇淋已蔚為流行。過去四個月來，公司已進行口味測試。[2] 這種內餡將在加州市場上試賣兩個月。兩個月後會決定是否對此產品增加生產。[3]

Meldane 說：「我們都知道洛杉磯地區是多元的，亞洲的口味在我們這裡越來越受歡迎。[4] 我們非常相信這個口味同樣會成功並最終受到大眾喜愛。」

A 155. 關於 Cookie Fantastic，文中提到了什麼？

(A) 它將推出新系列的餅乾。　　　　(B) 它由 Adrian Meldane 創辦。

(C) 它是洛杉磯最大的餅乾公司。　　　(D) 它專賣亞洲口味產品。

▶說明 文章第一句話就提到 Cookie Fantastic 月底將在加州市場上推出新口味的餅乾，故正確答案為 (A)。

C 156. 以下何者並非 Adrian Meldane 注意到的事？

(A) 加州有許多華裔美國人。　　　　　(B) 奶茶冰淇淋已蔚為流行。

(C) 奶茶口味的餅乾在加州非常流行。　(D) 奶茶在華裔美國人的社區之外也很流行。

▶說明 文末提到 Adrian Meldane 相信未來奶茶口味的餅乾終會受到歡迎，這是對未來的期望，而非現在注意到的事實，故選 (C)。

B 157. 以下這句話最適合放在文中哪個位置？

「這些測試顯示來自不同背景的人們都喜歡奶茶口味的夾心內餡。」

(A) [1]　　　　　**(B) [2]**　　　　　(C) [3]　　　　　(D) [4]

▶說明 這句話的主詞為 these tests，可推知前文必曾提到 tests，而 [2] 的前文正好說到公司進行的口味測試，且 [2] 的後一句主詞為 the filling，正是指題目上這句話的重點 milk tea -flavored cream filling，故答案為 (B)。

請參考以下的備忘錄回答**第 158 題至 160 題**。

收件人：全體員工

寄件人：人力資源部

日期：十一月一日

管理部門已注意到有太多員工的午休時間超過三十分鐘的限制。管理部門想提醒員工，當他們休息超過表定的午休時間，會讓其他員工無法休息。這也降低我們管理超市各部門的效率。

管理部門知道超市外沒有太多地方可以買午餐。因此，我們要施行兩項措施以解決此問題。其一是休息室將會放置冰箱和微波爐，歡迎所有員工使用。不過，員工的名字必須清楚標示在他們放進冰箱的食物和飲料上。另外，不可在沒有經過門市經理許可的情況下將食物在冰箱擺放過夜。

第二項措施是公司每天會為有意願的員工訂購附近餐廳的餐點。每天早上當天的菜單會被貼在休息室。員工只需要寫下他們想訂購的餐點並在午餐時間之前交錢給門市經理。

並且，我們超市的所有食物商品依舊有七五折員工價。謝謝你們的配合，幫助我們的超市成為這地區最好的超市。

Chloe Morgan

C 158. 備忘錄中提到的問題是什麼？

(A) 員工在午餐時間沒有東西吃。　　　(B) 沒有足夠的員工做完所有工作。

(C) 許多員工的午休時間超過表定時間。　(D) 有些員工常常忘記付午餐錢。

▶說明 備忘錄的第一段第一句提到太多員工的午休時間超過三十分鐘的限制，故正確答案為 (C)。

D 159. 根據備忘錄，員工未經門市經理許可不能做什麼？

(A) 走出超市去買午餐　　　　　　　　　　(B) 向附近餐廳訂餐點

(C) 使用休息室的微波爐　　　　　　　　**(D) 將食物在冰箱擺放過夜**

▶說明 備忘錄的第二段最後一句提到不可在沒有經過門市經理許可的情況下將食物在冰箱擺放過夜，故正確答案為 (D)。

B 160. Chloe Morgan 最可能是什麼身分？

(A) 門市經理　　　　**(B) 人資經理**　　　　(C) 採購經理　　　　(D) 員工餐廳經理

▶說明 備忘錄最後的署名為 Chloe Morgan，而開頭的寄件人為人資部門，故 (B) 人資經理為合理的答案。

請參考以下的線上討論內容回答**第 161 題至 164 題**。

Ethan：[十三點二十二分] 林先生的訂單進度如何？
Zoe：[十三點二十六分] 你是說要寄去臺灣的畫圖用具嗎？
Ethan：[十三點二十八分] 是的。電腦顯示它還沒寄出，雖然我們十二號就收到訂單了。
Zoe：[十三點三十二分] 顏料四天前就準備好了，也就是二十二號。訂單還沒寄出嗎？Lucas 可能知道問題出在哪裡。
Lucas：[十三點三十七分] 我剛發現問題出在哪。林先生也要六種美術紙，但其中有兩種缺貨。不過我們今天剛收到供應商送來的大批貨物。在碼頭的工作人員目前正在卸貨。根據貨物標籤，林先生需要的東西應該就在這批貨物中。
Ethan：[十三點四十分] 如果它們在這批貨物中，我們預計何時可以將訂單寄出？林先生想知道是何時。
Lucas：[十三點四十五分] 假設其他事情都已安排妥當，六七點前應該可以準備寄出。
Zoe：[十三點四十九分] 箱子都準備好了。美術紙一到我們就可以立刻將它們寄出。

B 161. 三人可能在何種公司工作？

(A) 貨運公司　　　　**(B) 美術用品公司**　　　(C) 紡織廠　　　　(D) 畫廊

▶說明 文中提到這家公司的客戶訂購了 "paints"、"art paper" 等物品，可推知這家公司是專門販售美術用品的公司，故正確答案為 (B)。

A 162. 何時接到訂單？

(A) 兩週前　　　　(B) 三週前　　　　(C) 四天前　　　　(D) 十天前

▶說明 文中提到十二號接到訂單，而四天前是二十二號，表示對話當下是二十六號，距離十二號為兩週，故正確答案為 (A)。

D 163. 訂單為何延誤？

(A) 天氣不好。　　(B) 訂貨單不見了。　　(C) 林先生修改訂單。**(D) 兩種美術紙缺貨。**

▶說明 Lucas 在 13:37 的留言提到 "Mr. Lin also wanted six kinds of art paper, but two of them were out of stock."，因此可以得知該筆訂單延遲出貨的原因是兩種美術用紙缺貨所造成的，故正確答案為 (D)。

B 164. 討論過後，訂單預期何時寄出？

(A) 現在　　　　**(B) 今晚**　　　　(C) 明天　　　　(D) 下週

▶說明 文末提到六七點前應該可以準備寄出，故正確答案為 (B)。

請參考以下的公告回答**第 165 題至 167 題**。

電腦室規定

1. 向圖書館員出示卡片以領取密碼。

2. 電腦室內禁止飲食。

3. 不可使用電腦超過一小時。

4. 禁止下載任何軟體或應用程式。

5. 進入電腦室前請脫鞋。

6. 為了尊重其他使用者，請使用耳機並將音量調小。

C 165. 人們最可能在何處看到這張公告？

(A) 在火車站　　　　(B) 在書店　　　　**(C) 在公共圖書館**　　(D) 在購物商場

▶說明 這篇文章是電腦室的使用規定，第一條規則提到圖書館員，因此可推知這應該是附屬於某個圖書館的電腦室，故正確答案為 (C)。

C 166. 電腦室中允許以下哪種行為？

(A) 喝茶　　　　　　(B) 下載遊戲　　　　**(C) 戴耳機看影片**　　(D) 穿著自己的鞋子

▶說明 第六條規則提到為了尊重其他使用者須使用耳機，因此戴耳機看影片並未違反任何一條規則，故正確答案為 (C)。

B 167. 一個人使用電腦最久可以多久？

(A) 三十分鐘　　　　**(B) 六十分鐘**　　　(C) 兩小時　　　　(D) 三小時

▶說明 第三條提到不可使用電腦超過一小時，故正確答案為 (B)。

請參考以下的電子郵件回答**第 168 題至 171 題**。

寄件人：Thomas Cooper <fitnesscourse@unbelievable.com>

收件人：Callie Scott <callie7931@pmail.com>

主旨：恭喜

日期：六月三十日

您好，

Unbelievable 健身中心恭喜您於本月完成我們的健身課程！我們相信您已有所學習、成長並變得更加強健。我們很高興見證您的改變。請幫我們填寫回饋單：http://unbelievable.fitnesscourse/feedback-form，這樣我們就會知道您對我們的課程及對本中心的想法。如果您於七月一日前填完回饋單，您將免費獲得運動毛巾一條。

保持健康從來不容易。我們希望這期課程的結束並非您訓練的結束，而是另一個開始。如果您想要身強體壯，請繼續和我們同行。我們下期課程將於七月八日開課。請於七月五日前完成報名。我們將再次提供給您充足的運動及仔細的指導。並且，由於您已經是本中心的會員，您享有下期課程八五折的優惠！

如果您對於新課程有任何疑問，請聯絡我們。看見我們所有的會員過著健康快樂的生活一直是我們最希望的事。請讓我們成為您一生的運動夥伴。

致上誠摯的問候，

Thomas Cooper
Unbelievable 健身中心

B 168. 這封電子郵件的目的為何？

(A) 宣傳工作機會   **(B) 推銷新的健身課程**

(C) 給予關於運動方式的建議   (D) 鼓勵想要減重的人

▶說明 信件內容主要在恭喜對方完成當期健身課程並鼓勵對方繼續上新課程，可知信件的主要目的是推銷新課程，故正確答案為 (B)。

C 169. 第二段第二行 "robust" 的字義最接近於

(A) 快樂的   (B) 苗條的   **(C) 健康的**   (D) 有前途的

▶說明 robust 一字出現的這句話表示要成為一個 robust 的人就請繼續參與健身中心的課程，而 robust 的前文提及 "To keep fit is never easy"，可推知 robust 的字義最接近健康的，故正確答案為 (C)。

B 170. 關於 Callie Scott，文中提及了什麼？

(A) 她已填完回饋單。   **(B) 她已有健身中心的會員資格。**

(C) 她正在尋找運動夥伴。   (D) 她從未上過任何健身課程。

▶說明 Callie Scott 為信件收件人，而信件第二段最後提到對方已經是本中心的會員，故正確答案為 (B)。

C 171. 報名截止日期為何時？

(A) 六月三十日   (B) 七月一日   **(C) 七月五日**   (D) 七月八日

▶說明 第二段提到要在七月五日前完成報名，故正確答案為 (C)。

請參考以下的信件回答**第 172 題至 175 題**。

Greeneville 出版社
328 Maple 街，春田，
麻薩諸塞州 01101
(820) 624–7800

Cameron Russell
302 Central 街
曼徹斯特，新罕布夏 03103

親愛的 Russell 先生，

我們很高興您考慮在我們公司下訂單。[1] 我們的許多語言學習書籍已獲得各種獎項，我們的法文學習叢書也受到世界各地許多讀者的讚賞。所有的作者、插畫家、設計師和這裡的員工都以我們如此的成果自豪。[2]

您會發現我們的許多書籍在過去兩年間都已更新，以確保它們保有最新的資訊並使用最新的語言學習法。此外，我們大部分的書籍都包含多種學習活動。[3] 我們還提供多項輔助資源，包括練習

本、DVD、光碟、和線上家教課程。

請看我附上的手冊。[4] 我相信它能幫助您選擇您要買的書籍。我也鼓勵您上我們的網站看看多種視聽學習資源的使用方式。如果您有任何進一步的問題，請隨時打電話或寄電子郵件給我們。

致上親切的問候，

Harper Powell
Greeneville 出版社

B 172. 這封信的目的為何？

    (A) 邀請作者寫新書　　　　　　　　　**(B) 提供書籍資訊**

    (C) 徵聘新老師　　　　　　　　　　　(D) 誇耀出版社的成就

    ▶說明 由信中內容可以得知，此封信主要是在針對潛在的客戶介紹該公司的書籍，因此正確答案為 (B)。

D 173. 信件的附件為何？

    (A) 聘雇合約　　　　(B) 訂單表格　　　　(C) 書籍試閱本　　　　**(D) 介紹書籍的手冊**

    ▶說明 在信中最後一段提到 "Please look at the guide I have enclosed. I am sure it will help you as you choose which books to buy"，可知在信中附上了該公司的書籍簡介手冊，故正確答案為 (D)。

A 174. 第二段第二行 "employ" 的字義最接近於

    (A) 使用　　　　　(B) 雇用　　　　　　(C) 發明　　　　　　(D) 改變

    ▶說明 由 employ 一字在信中的前後文意來判斷，此時的字意應為「使用、利用」，故正確答案為 (A)。

C 175. 以下這句話最適合放在文中哪個位置？

    「它們都被設計來激發不同程度的學習者學習並思考。」

    (A) [1]　　　　　　　(B) [2]　　　　　　　**(C) [3]**　　　　　　(D) [4]

    ▶說明 由句意可知，此句的主詞 They 是可以促進學習的事物，而信中第二段提到各種學習資源，因此最適合的地方為 [3]，故答案為 (C)。

請參考以下的清單和電子郵件回答**第 176 題至 180 題**。

CHIESA Supply 公司

顧客姓名：James Thompson

顧客地址：布里斯本市 Sunnybank Hills，Mains 路 794 號

日期：五月十二日

商品編號	描述	數量	單價 (澳幣)	總額 (澳幣)
RT 19855	藍白地毯 195 公分×250 公分	1,500	$100	$150,000
RT 19854	大床 152 公分×203 公分	20	$300	$6,000
RT 19853	茶几 55 公分×55 公分×45 公分	140	$120	$16,800
RT 19852	組合式窗間矮几 45 公分×60 公分×55 公分	130	$130	$16,900
總金額				$189,700

收件人：thompson@sevenstarhotel.com
寄件人：gonzales@chiesasupply.com
主旨：為 Thompson 先生的訂貨問題致歉
日期：五月十五日

親愛的 Thompson 先生：

我們必須向您道歉。我們得知送到您飯店的貨品有一些問題：地毯比您訂的少了四條，且有五張組合式的窗間矮几的零件受損。我們為這些問題致歉。

今天早上我們已寄送四條地毯。至於窗間矮几的零件，我們很遺憾要告訴您零件缺貨並且矮几也已經停產了。我們將依五張矮几的原價退款給您。

如果關於您的訂貨有任何問題，請隨時與我們聯絡。

致上誠摯的問候，

業務代表 Andrea Gonzales
07-1234-5678
CHIESA Supply 公司

C 176. 為什麼 Gonzales 小姐寫信給 Thompson 先生？

(A) 訂購一些家具　　　(B) 促銷新產品　　　**(C) 致歉**　　　　　(D) 詢問資訊

▶說明 由信件主旨和內文第一句話可得知寫信的目的是要致歉，故正確答案為 (C)。

B 177. 四張地毯是何時被寄去 Thompson 先生的飯店？

(A) 昨天　　　　　**(B) 今天早上**　　　(C) 今天下午　　　(D) 今天晚上

▶說明 信中第二段第一句提到四張地毯於今天早上寄出，故正確答案為 (B)。

A 178. 關於窗間矮几，文中提到了什麼？

(A) 零件無法取得。　　　　　　　　(B) 它們被駕駛員損壞。

(C) 它們正被製造中。　　　　　　　　(D) 它們被送錯地方。

▶說明 信中第二段第二句提到窗間矮几的零件缺貨並且矮几也已經停產了，故正確答案為 (A)。

D 179. CHIESA Supply 公司要退給 Thompson 先生多少錢？

(A) 四百元　　　　(B) 五百二十元　　　(C) 六百元　　　**(D) 六百五十元**

▶說明 信中第二段最後一句提到 CHIESA Supply 公司要依五張矮几的原價退款給 Thompson 先生，而根據 Thompson 先生的訂單，每張矮几單價為一百三十元，五張即為六百五十元，故正確答案為 (D)。

D 180. 地毯的尺寸為何？

(A) 45 公分 × 60 公分　　　　　　　(B) 55 公分 × 55 公分

(C) 152 公分 × 203 公分　　　　　　**(D) 195 公分 × 250 公分**

▶說明 根據訂單的商品描述欄位，地毯的尺寸為 195 公分 ×250 公分，故正確答案為 (D)。

請參考以下的網頁和信件回答**第 181 題至 185 題**。

---

http://www.jobseeker.com/

徵商業訓練顧問

公司名稱：Hiller Heiman

職位：大型國際企業正在尋找經驗豐富的商界人士來擔任商業訓練講師及顧問。

應徵條件：應徵者須有勤勉的工作態度與研究精神，並具備可靠的職業操守，且善於處理和客戶
之間的人際關係。

工作內容：工作包含在大型訓練會上發言、引導並激勵創業者成功設立公司。顧問將需要每月參
與一次內部訓練課程 (即在職訓練) 並對外為商界人士安排訓練課程。

到職日期：一週內

親愛的人事經理：

我的名字是 Johnny McBeth。 我寫這封信是想應徵商業訓練顧問， 此職缺這個月在報紙上刊登
過。

我在相關領域的經驗如下： 我在上海市的一家貿易公司工作了十五年。 我曾是 Hong Kong
Shanghai 貿易有限公司的業務代表，這是一家將軟體出口到香港的中國本地企業。在那裡工作
三年後我就晉升為經理。我也曾擔任兼職商業顧問十年的時間。我為當地企業安排工作坊和商業
訓練課程。

我很有信心能勝任這個職位並保證讓你們的商業訓練課程及工作坊帶給客戶最大的益處。如果您
覺得我適合這項職位，請最晚於四月十二日下週四前聯絡我。我只有在那天之前有空參加面試。

非常謝謝您。

Johnny McBeth

B 181. 關於 Hiller Heiman，文中提到了什麼？

(A) 它的總部設在上海市。　　　　　　　　**(B) 它提供商業訓練課程。**

(C) 它正在招募業務代表。　　　　　　　　(D) 大部分的客戶是秘書。

▶說明 網頁上提到所招募的商業訓練顧問的工作內容是為商界人士安排訓練課程， 可知
Hiller Heiman 公司提供商業課程，因此正確答案為 (B)。

D 182. 根據網頁，成功的應徵者會被要求做什麼事情？

(A) 協助出口軟體到香港　　　　　　　　(B) 在大型商業展覽會上發言

(C) 參與國際會議　　　　　　　　　　　**(D) 給予關於如何創業的建議**

▶說明 網頁上提到應徵的工作內容包括引導並激勵創業者成功設立公司， 故正確答案為
(D)。

C 183. 什麼很可能讓 McBeth 先生適合這項職位？

(A) 他曾擔任研究員。   (B) 他是經驗豐富的建築工人。

(C) 他有許多擔任商業顧問的經驗。   (D) 他在貿易公司負責運貨的業務。

▶說明 McBeth 先生在信中第一段提到自己要應徵的是商業訓練顧問，第二段則提到自己有許多相關領域的工作經驗，其中包含曾擔任兼職商業顧問十年的時間，故正確答案為 (C)。

A 184. 如果 McBeth 先生被錄用，他最有可能何時就職？

(A) 四月   (B) 五月   (C) 六月   (D) 七月

▶說明 網頁上載明到職日期為一週內，而信中 McBeth 先生表示自己只有在四月十二前有空面試，由此可推知如果他被錄用，應會在四月就職，故正確答案為 (A)。

B 185. 信中第三段第三行 "available" 的字義最接近於

(A) 簡單的   **(B) 有空的**   (C) 便利的   (D) 可得到的

▶說明 信中最後一句的句意為 McBeth 先生只有在那天之前「有空」參加面試，故正確答案為 (B)。

請參考以下的摘要、時刻表及電子郵件回答**第 186 題至 190 題**。

《快樂的兔子》與《甜甜圈之王》	作者：Hazel Tryniski

◆《快樂的兔子》：一隻兔子在看到人類的快樂與悲傷後決定當一隻快樂的兔子。在這個故事裡，所有寵物都會說話，並且牠們常有風趣的言論。

◆《甜甜圈之王》：Dominic 是一位麵包師傅。有一天他遇見一位陌生人，他帶 Dominic 來到一個神秘的國度，展開一場不可思議的魔法之旅。

PG2 電臺
黃金時段廣播節目表
三月二十七日 星期二

十八點整─**今晚運動賽事**：城市裡最熱門的運動談話節目。來聽我們的主持人 Ryan Jackson 與本地體育界優秀的運動員及其他來賓談論運動賽事吧！

十九點整─**作家角落**：今晚的來賓 Carson Tryniski 將談談他對於他母親所寫的兩部小說的想法。他也會談到彙編及出版他母親對於小說虛構場景的筆記。

二十點整─**讓我們來談政治**：Sean Watson 會談談本地政治。聽聽節目並打電話進來。讓我們的城市聽見你的聲音。

收件人：listenerfeedback@pg2radio.com
寄件人：ameliamyers@wmail.com
日期：三月二十八日
主旨：關於作家角落

我從大學時期至今已經固定收聽 PG2 電臺三十年了。「作家角落」一直是我最喜歡的節目。我熱愛閱讀，聽作家談論他們的作品總是很吸引人。

昨天的節目對我有特別的意義。我從小就是 Hazel Tryniski 的頭號粉絲。我喜歡她所創造的虛構世界。雖然她已不在人世，聽她的兒子談論她的小說仍然很有意思。

謝謝你們這麼棒的節目。

Amelia Myers

B 186. 誰是 Carson Tryniski？

(A) Hazel Tryniski 的丈夫　　　　　　　　**(B) Hazel Tryniski 的兒子**

(C) 「作家角落」的主持人　　　　　　　　(D) 《快樂的兔子》的作者

▶說明 時刻表中提到 Carson Tryniski 將在「作家角落」談談他對於母親所寫的兩部小說的想法，而電子郵件提到 Hazel Tryniski 的兒子在節目上談論她的小說，故可推知正確答案為 (B)。

D 187. 為什麼 Hazel Tryniski 沒有上這個廣播節目？

(A) 她太忙了。　　　(B) 她現在在國外。　　(C) 她兒子不准。　　**(D) 她已經辭世。**

▶說明 在電子郵件第二段中，Amelia Myers 提到 Hazel Tryniski 已不在人世，但聽她的兒子談論她的小說仍然很有意思，故可推知正確答案為 (D)。

A 188. 如果你對籃球有興趣，你應該要在三月二十七日何時收聽 PG2 電臺？

(A) 十八點整　　　(B) 十九點整　　　(C) 二十點整　　　(D) 二十一點整

▶說明 根據時刻表，18:00 的節目是 Sports Tonight，因此如果喜歡體育類的節目，應該要在 18:00 時收聽這個節目，故正確答案為 (A)。

C 189. 關於 Myers 女士所喜歡的虛構世界，何者最有可能為真？

(A) 世界由魔法師統治。　　　　　　　　(B) 世界裡到處是麵包店。

(C) 在那裡動物會說話及思考。　　　　(D) 在那裡成人會說好笑的話。

▶說明 根據電子郵件第二段可知 Myers 女士所喜歡的虛構世界是指 Hazel Tryniski 在小說中所創造的世界，而根據小說摘要，在《快樂的兔子》的世界裡，寵物會說話並且常有風趣的言論，故可推知正確答案為 (C)。

D 190. Myers 女士可能的歲數為何？

(A) 十幾歲　　　　(B) 二十歲初　　　　(C) 四十歲初　　　**(D) 五十歲初**

▶說明 電子郵件第一段提到 Myers 女士從大學時期至今已經固定收聽 PG2 電臺三十年，因此可以反推她現在的年紀應該大約是五十初，故正確答案為 (D)。

請參考以下的產品資訊、線上評論及回覆回答**第 191 題至 195 題**。

Backstrong 背包
Bikeback 系列

尺寸	價格	可供挑選的顏色
二十公升	$29.99	藍、綠、紅、黃
三十公升	$33.99	紅、黃、黑
四十公升	$38.99	藍、黃、黑、粉紅
五十公升	$42.99	黃、黑、橘

細節：

* 一個大隔間

* 固定筆記型電腦於大隔間的帶子

* 一個放小物品的較小的夾層，有能放筆、鑰匙、眼鏡等的口袋

* 一個底部夾層
* 兩條背帶，減輕您背部的壓力
* 兩個側邊口袋，供放置水壺或雨傘

---

https://www.backstrongbackpacks.com/Products/Bikeback/reviews
十二月二十九日

我聖誕節剛收到一個黃色、四十公升的 Bikeback 背包。我很興奮收到朋友送的這個禮物。我大致上對這個產品滿意。我喜歡固定我的筆記型電腦的帶子，因為我常需要帶它去辦公室。此外，我不用再擔心眼鏡要放哪裡了。顏色是黃色的也讓汽車駕駛能在晚上很容易的看到我。

不過我有點擔心它的耐用性。它看起來不太堅固。我對包包通常很粗魯，大部分我用的包包壽命都不會超過一年。我希望這個背包能成為例外，不過我還是有點擔心。我希望這是我杞人憂天。

Charlie Fisher

---

https://www.backstrongbackpacks.com/Products/Bikeback/replies
一月二日

親愛的 Fisher 先生：

謝謝您給我們關於您的聖誕禮物的回饋。我們理解您對耐用性的擔憂。它是一個很輕量的背包。這是因為它使用業界最新的輕量材質。但它其實是很堅固耐用的。它在測試階段通過了現實生活中劇烈使用的情境。

每個 Bikeback 背包都有一年保固。如果有任何其他問題，請聯絡我們。

Marie Olson
Backstrong 背包客戶服務部

B 191. Bikeback 系列提供幾種尺寸的產品？

(A) 二種　　　　　**(B) 四種**　　　　(C) 六種　　　　(D) 十四種

▶說明 由產品資訊可知該系列總共提供四種尺寸的背包，故正確答案為 (B)。

A 192. Fisher 先生是如何得到他的背包的？

(A) 背包是聖誕禮物　(B) 背包是生日禮物　(C) 從抽獎拿到　　(D) 背包是獎勵

▶說明 根據線上評論第一段，Fisher 先生在聖誕節收到一個 Bikeback 背包作為禮物，故正確答案為 (A)。

D 193. Fisher 先生說「我不用再擔心眼鏡要放哪裡了」是什麼意思？

(A) 他可以把眼鏡放在背包的大隔間。　　(B) 他可以用背包的帶子固定眼鏡。

(C) 他可以把眼鏡放在背包的側邊口袋。　**(D) 他可以把眼鏡放在背包較小的夾層。**

▶說明 Fisher 先生在線上評論第一段表示對 Bikeback 背包的想法時，提到「我不用再擔心眼鏡要放哪裡了」，可知這句話是針對 Bikeback 背包的看法之一，而產品資訊中提到

Bikeback 背包的較小的夾層裡面有能夠放置筆、鑰匙、眼鏡等的口袋，故正確答案為 (D)。

C 194. Fisher 先生的背包價格為何？

(A) $29.99　　　　(B) $33.99　　　　**(C) $38.99**　　　　(D) $42.99

▶說明 根據線上評論，Fisher 先生的背包是黃色、四十公升的 Bikeback 背包，而根據產品資訊可知該款背包價格為 $38.99，故正確答案為 (C)。

B 195. Olson 女士給 Fisher 先生什麼保證？

(A) 公司會給他一個新的背包。　　　　**(B) 背包有一年保固。**

(C) 這些背包會繼續販售很長一段時間。　　(D) 黃色是最熱門的選擇。

▶說明 Ms. Olson 回覆的第二段提到每個 Bikeback 背包都有一年保固，故正確答案為 (B)。

請參考以下的電子郵件、公告及文章回答**第 196 題至 200 題**。

收件人：Ruby Brown

寄件人：Sharon Smith

日期：十二月十八日

主旨：團體照

親愛的 Brown 先生：

這封信是要確認下週一早上在貴公司的拍照時段。此時段大約三十分鐘。我們會在貴公司的大門拍照，並會拍數張照片。依您所要求的，全體員工將會一起入鏡，之後再拍各部門的照片。

若您有任何問題，請盡快讓我知道。週一見。

祝好，

Sharon Smith

Venus 照相館

所有員工請注意！我有振奮人心的消息要告訴你們。我們今年被認可為本市最佳企業。這是我們公司第一次獲得此項榮譽。這也是全體員工辛勤工作的證明。

下週一早上九點半將會拍團體照。全體員工都將入鏡。照片會在公司大樓門口拍攝，背景是很大的公司標誌。

下週一早上九點半請準備好，以便盡快完成拍照。

　　Lincoln Great Spirit 公司最近被公布獲得了本市年度最佳企業的獎項。這家去年慶祝五十週年的公司是第一次獲得這項榮譽。

　　「我六年前來到這裡時，這裡問題很多，」公司負責人 Graham 先生說，「但因為員工的努力及客戶的支持，我們得以讓這家企業改頭換面。」

　　「Graham 先生藉著他無限的熱情和追求進步的創新想法已完全扭轉了局面。」 公司經理 Ruby Brown 說。

C 196. Smith 女士寫信給誰？

(A) 設計師   (B) 記者   **(C) 公司經理**   (D) 公司負責人

▶說明 第一篇電子郵件的收件人是 Ruby Brown，而第三篇文章最後提到 Ruby Brown 是公司的經理，故正確答案為 (C)。

B 197. 拍照時段可能會何時結束？

(A) 九點   **(B) 十點**   (C) 十一點   (D) 十二點

▶說明 公告中提到拍照時段於九點半開始，而電子郵件提到拍照時段大約三十分鐘，也就是大約十點結束，故正確答案為 (B)。

C 198. 團體照的背景將是什麼？

(A) 大樓門口前的草坪   (B) 年度最佳企業的獎牌

(C) 公司的標誌   (D) 電影明星的海報

▶說明 公告第二段的最後一句提到拍照背景是很大的公司標誌，故正確答案為 (C)。

A 199. Graham 先生在這間公司多久了？

(A) 六年   (B) 八年   (C) 十年   (D) 五十年

▶說明 在第三篇文章的第二段，Graham 先生提到他六年前來到這家公司，故正確答案為 (A)。

D 200. 關於 Lincoln Great Spirit 公司，文中提及了什麼？

(A) 員工通常九點上班。   (B) 它多次獲獎。

(C) 它今年獲利極高。   **(D) 它已超過五十年。**

▶說明 第三篇文章提到 Lincoln Great Spirit 公司在去年慶祝了五十週年，故正確答案為 (D)。

新多益黃金互動 16 週：進階篇模擬試題分數換算表

Listening Test		Reading Test	
答對題數	預測分數	答對題數	預測分數
100	495	100	495
98	490	98	475
95	485	95	455
92	470	92	450
89	465	89	430
86	450	86	410
81	425	81	385
79	420	79	375
76	400	76	355
71	385	71	350
66	375	66	330
64	350	64	315
61	330	61	295
59	325	59	285
56	305	56	265
54	290	54	260
51	270	51	240
49	260	49	230
46	240	46	210
44	225	44	200
41	210	41	180
38	190	38	170
36	170	36	150
34	155	34	140
31	135	31	120
28	125	28	115
26	105	26	95
24	100	24	70
21	80	21	55
18	75	18	50
16	55	16	40
13	50	13	35
11	30	11	20
6	10	6	10
0	5	0	5

（此分數換算表僅供參考，實際考試分數以量尺分數計算。）

新多益黃金互動 16 週：進階篇模擬試題 ANSWER SHEET

聽力測驗 LISTENING

1 Ⓐ Ⓑ Ⓒ Ⓓ	26 Ⓐ Ⓑ Ⓒ Ⓓ	51 Ⓐ Ⓑ Ⓒ Ⓓ	76 Ⓐ Ⓑ Ⓒ Ⓓ	
2 Ⓐ Ⓑ Ⓒ Ⓓ	27 Ⓐ Ⓑ Ⓒ Ⓓ	52 Ⓐ Ⓑ Ⓒ Ⓓ	77 Ⓐ Ⓑ Ⓒ Ⓓ	
3 Ⓐ Ⓑ Ⓒ Ⓓ	28 Ⓐ Ⓑ Ⓒ Ⓓ	53 Ⓐ Ⓑ Ⓒ Ⓓ	78 Ⓐ Ⓑ Ⓒ Ⓓ	
4 Ⓐ Ⓑ Ⓒ Ⓓ	29 Ⓐ Ⓑ Ⓒ Ⓓ	54 Ⓐ Ⓑ Ⓒ Ⓓ	79 Ⓐ Ⓑ Ⓒ Ⓓ	
5 Ⓐ Ⓑ Ⓒ Ⓓ	30 Ⓐ Ⓑ Ⓒ Ⓓ	55 Ⓐ Ⓑ Ⓒ Ⓓ	80 Ⓐ Ⓑ Ⓒ Ⓓ	
6 Ⓐ Ⓑ Ⓒ Ⓓ	31 Ⓐ Ⓑ Ⓒ Ⓓ	56 Ⓐ Ⓑ Ⓒ Ⓓ	81 Ⓐ Ⓑ Ⓒ Ⓓ	
7 Ⓐ Ⓑ Ⓒ	32 Ⓐ Ⓑ Ⓒ Ⓓ	57 Ⓐ Ⓑ Ⓒ Ⓓ	82 Ⓐ Ⓑ Ⓒ Ⓓ	
8 Ⓐ Ⓑ Ⓒ	33 Ⓐ Ⓑ Ⓒ Ⓓ	58 Ⓐ Ⓑ Ⓒ Ⓓ	83 Ⓐ Ⓑ Ⓒ Ⓓ	
9 Ⓐ Ⓑ Ⓒ	34 Ⓐ Ⓑ Ⓒ Ⓓ	59 Ⓐ Ⓑ Ⓒ Ⓓ	84 Ⓐ Ⓑ Ⓒ Ⓓ	
10 Ⓐ Ⓑ Ⓒ	35 Ⓐ Ⓑ Ⓒ Ⓓ	60 Ⓐ Ⓑ Ⓒ Ⓓ	85 Ⓐ Ⓑ Ⓒ Ⓓ	
11 Ⓐ Ⓑ Ⓒ	36 Ⓐ Ⓑ Ⓒ Ⓓ	61 Ⓐ Ⓑ Ⓒ Ⓓ	86 Ⓐ Ⓑ Ⓒ Ⓓ	
12 Ⓐ Ⓑ Ⓒ	37 Ⓐ Ⓑ Ⓒ Ⓓ	62 Ⓐ Ⓑ Ⓒ Ⓓ	87 Ⓐ Ⓑ Ⓒ Ⓓ	
13 Ⓐ Ⓑ Ⓒ	38 Ⓐ Ⓑ Ⓒ Ⓓ	63 Ⓐ Ⓑ Ⓒ Ⓓ	88 Ⓐ Ⓑ Ⓒ Ⓓ	
14 Ⓐ Ⓑ Ⓒ	39 Ⓐ Ⓑ Ⓒ Ⓓ	64 Ⓐ Ⓑ Ⓒ Ⓓ	89 Ⓐ Ⓑ Ⓒ Ⓓ	
15 Ⓐ Ⓑ Ⓒ	40 Ⓐ Ⓑ Ⓒ Ⓓ	65 Ⓐ Ⓑ Ⓒ Ⓓ	90 Ⓐ Ⓑ Ⓒ Ⓓ	
16 Ⓐ Ⓑ Ⓒ	41 Ⓐ Ⓑ Ⓒ Ⓓ	66 Ⓐ Ⓑ Ⓒ Ⓓ	91 Ⓐ Ⓑ Ⓒ Ⓓ	
17 Ⓐ Ⓑ Ⓒ	42 Ⓐ Ⓑ Ⓒ Ⓓ	67 Ⓐ Ⓑ Ⓒ Ⓓ	92 Ⓐ Ⓑ Ⓒ Ⓓ	
18 Ⓐ Ⓑ Ⓒ	43 Ⓐ Ⓑ Ⓒ Ⓓ	68 Ⓐ Ⓑ Ⓒ Ⓓ	93 Ⓐ Ⓑ Ⓒ Ⓓ	
19 Ⓐ Ⓑ Ⓒ	44 Ⓐ Ⓑ Ⓒ Ⓓ	69 Ⓐ Ⓑ Ⓒ Ⓓ	94 Ⓐ Ⓑ Ⓒ Ⓓ	
20 Ⓐ Ⓑ Ⓒ	45 Ⓐ Ⓑ Ⓒ Ⓓ	70 Ⓐ Ⓑ Ⓒ Ⓓ	95 Ⓐ Ⓑ Ⓒ Ⓓ	
21 Ⓐ Ⓑ Ⓒ	46 Ⓐ Ⓑ Ⓒ Ⓓ	71 Ⓐ Ⓑ Ⓒ Ⓓ	96 Ⓐ Ⓑ Ⓒ Ⓓ	
22 Ⓐ Ⓑ Ⓒ	47 Ⓐ Ⓑ Ⓒ Ⓓ	72 Ⓐ Ⓑ Ⓒ Ⓓ	97 Ⓐ Ⓑ Ⓒ Ⓓ	
23 Ⓐ Ⓑ Ⓒ	48 Ⓐ Ⓑ Ⓒ Ⓓ	73 Ⓐ Ⓑ Ⓒ Ⓓ	98 Ⓐ Ⓑ Ⓒ Ⓓ	
24 Ⓐ Ⓑ Ⓒ	49 Ⓐ Ⓑ Ⓒ Ⓓ	74 Ⓐ Ⓑ Ⓒ Ⓓ	99 Ⓐ Ⓑ Ⓒ Ⓓ	
25 Ⓐ Ⓑ Ⓒ	50 Ⓐ Ⓑ Ⓒ Ⓓ	75 Ⓐ Ⓑ Ⓒ Ⓓ	100 Ⓐ Ⓑ Ⓒ Ⓓ	

閱讀測驗 READING

101 Ⓐ Ⓑ Ⓒ Ⓓ	126 Ⓐ Ⓑ Ⓒ Ⓓ	151 Ⓐ Ⓑ Ⓒ Ⓓ	176 Ⓐ Ⓑ Ⓒ Ⓓ
102 Ⓐ Ⓑ Ⓒ Ⓓ	127 Ⓐ Ⓑ Ⓒ Ⓓ	152 Ⓐ Ⓑ Ⓒ Ⓓ	177 Ⓐ Ⓑ Ⓒ Ⓓ
103 Ⓐ Ⓑ Ⓒ Ⓓ	128 Ⓐ Ⓑ Ⓒ Ⓓ	153 Ⓐ Ⓑ Ⓒ Ⓓ	178 Ⓐ Ⓑ Ⓒ Ⓓ
104 Ⓐ Ⓑ Ⓒ Ⓓ	129 Ⓐ Ⓑ Ⓒ Ⓓ	154 Ⓐ Ⓑ Ⓒ Ⓓ	179 Ⓐ Ⓑ Ⓒ Ⓓ
105 Ⓐ Ⓑ Ⓒ Ⓓ	130 Ⓐ Ⓑ Ⓒ Ⓓ	155 Ⓐ Ⓑ Ⓒ Ⓓ	180 Ⓐ Ⓑ Ⓒ Ⓓ
106 Ⓐ Ⓑ Ⓒ Ⓓ	131 Ⓐ Ⓑ Ⓒ Ⓓ	156 Ⓐ Ⓑ Ⓒ Ⓓ	181 Ⓐ Ⓑ Ⓒ Ⓓ
107 Ⓐ Ⓑ Ⓒ Ⓓ	132 Ⓐ Ⓑ Ⓒ Ⓓ	157 Ⓐ Ⓑ Ⓒ Ⓓ	182 Ⓐ Ⓑ Ⓒ Ⓓ
108 Ⓐ Ⓑ Ⓒ Ⓓ	133 Ⓐ Ⓑ Ⓒ Ⓓ	158 Ⓐ Ⓑ Ⓒ Ⓓ	183 Ⓐ Ⓑ Ⓒ Ⓓ
109 Ⓐ Ⓑ Ⓒ Ⓓ	134 Ⓐ Ⓑ Ⓒ Ⓓ	159 Ⓐ Ⓑ Ⓒ Ⓓ	184 Ⓐ Ⓑ Ⓒ Ⓓ
110 Ⓐ Ⓑ Ⓒ Ⓓ	135 Ⓐ Ⓑ Ⓒ Ⓓ	160 Ⓐ Ⓑ Ⓒ Ⓓ	185 Ⓐ Ⓑ Ⓒ Ⓓ
111 Ⓐ Ⓑ Ⓒ Ⓓ	136 Ⓐ Ⓑ Ⓒ Ⓓ	161 Ⓐ Ⓑ Ⓒ Ⓓ	186 Ⓐ Ⓑ Ⓒ Ⓓ
112 Ⓐ Ⓑ Ⓒ Ⓓ	137 Ⓐ Ⓑ Ⓒ Ⓓ	162 Ⓐ Ⓑ Ⓒ Ⓓ	187 Ⓐ Ⓑ Ⓒ Ⓓ
113 Ⓐ Ⓑ Ⓒ Ⓓ	138 Ⓐ Ⓑ Ⓒ Ⓓ	163 Ⓐ Ⓑ Ⓒ Ⓓ	188 Ⓐ Ⓑ Ⓒ Ⓓ
114 Ⓐ Ⓑ Ⓒ Ⓓ	139 Ⓐ Ⓑ Ⓒ Ⓓ	164 Ⓐ Ⓑ Ⓒ Ⓓ	189 Ⓐ Ⓑ Ⓒ Ⓓ
115 Ⓐ Ⓑ Ⓒ Ⓓ	140 Ⓐ Ⓑ Ⓒ Ⓓ	165 Ⓐ Ⓑ Ⓒ Ⓓ	190 Ⓐ Ⓑ Ⓒ Ⓓ
116 Ⓐ Ⓑ Ⓒ Ⓓ	141 Ⓐ Ⓑ Ⓒ Ⓓ	166 Ⓐ Ⓑ Ⓒ Ⓓ	191 Ⓐ Ⓑ Ⓒ Ⓓ
117 Ⓐ Ⓑ Ⓒ Ⓓ	142 Ⓐ Ⓑ Ⓒ Ⓓ	167 Ⓐ Ⓑ Ⓒ Ⓓ	192 Ⓐ Ⓑ Ⓒ Ⓓ
118 Ⓐ Ⓑ Ⓒ Ⓓ	143 Ⓐ Ⓑ Ⓒ Ⓓ	168 Ⓐ Ⓑ Ⓒ Ⓓ	193 Ⓐ Ⓑ Ⓒ Ⓓ
119 Ⓐ Ⓑ Ⓒ Ⓓ	144 Ⓐ Ⓑ Ⓒ Ⓓ	169 Ⓐ Ⓑ Ⓒ Ⓓ	194 Ⓐ Ⓑ Ⓒ Ⓓ
120 Ⓐ Ⓑ Ⓒ Ⓓ	145 Ⓐ Ⓑ Ⓒ Ⓓ	170 Ⓐ Ⓑ Ⓒ Ⓓ	195 Ⓐ Ⓑ Ⓒ Ⓓ
121 Ⓐ Ⓑ Ⓒ Ⓓ	146 Ⓐ Ⓑ Ⓒ Ⓓ	171 Ⓐ Ⓑ Ⓒ Ⓓ	196 Ⓐ Ⓑ Ⓒ Ⓓ
122 Ⓐ Ⓑ Ⓒ Ⓓ	147 Ⓐ Ⓑ Ⓒ Ⓓ	172 Ⓐ Ⓑ Ⓒ Ⓓ	197 Ⓐ Ⓑ Ⓒ Ⓓ
123 Ⓐ Ⓑ Ⓒ Ⓓ	148 Ⓐ Ⓑ Ⓒ Ⓓ	173 Ⓐ Ⓑ Ⓒ Ⓓ	198 Ⓐ Ⓑ Ⓒ Ⓓ
124 Ⓐ Ⓑ Ⓒ Ⓓ	149 Ⓐ Ⓑ Ⓒ Ⓓ	174 Ⓐ Ⓑ Ⓒ Ⓓ	199 Ⓐ Ⓑ Ⓒ Ⓓ
125 Ⓐ Ⓑ Ⓒ Ⓓ	150 Ⓐ Ⓑ Ⓒ Ⓓ	175 Ⓐ Ⓑ Ⓒ Ⓓ	200 Ⓐ Ⓑ Ⓒ Ⓓ